THE

BARRE.... ....ɜ #4

JORDAN FORD

FLP

Cover art (copyright) by Emily Wittig Designs & Photography
https://www.facebook.com/emilywittigdesigns/

ISBN: 978-1-99-115132-2 (Paperback)
ISBN: 978-1-99-115133-9 (Kindle)

Forever Love Publishing Ltd
www.foreverlovepublishing.com

I dedicate this book to anyone who has had to forgive someone. It takes both strength and courage to overcome an emotional wound.

"The weak can never forgive. Forgiveness is the attribute of the strong." ~ Mahatma Ghandi

ONE HEAVENLY PHONE CALL

Jake

THE RAIN IS POURING OUTSIDE, hitting my skin. I blink against the spots, trying to clear my vision, but maybe it's not rain that's blinding me. Maybe it's tears. I don't know.

It's cold.

Icy.

My body is jostled as the pickup truck hits a pothole too fast. Hard metal digs into my back—a spike of pain that's completely different to the one in my chest. Grandpa Ray's head is cradled in my lap. I rest my hand on the top of his gray hair, unable to ignore the damp seeping through the towel, soaking into my jeans. That's not rain. It's not tears.

My stomach roils.

Blood.

Too much blood.

"Please don't die. Please." I grip his sodden shirt, lightly shaking him. "Open your eyes," I whimper.

But he won't.

Grandpa has been unconscious since the moment his head smacked into the brick around the fireplace.

Fury at my father sweeps through me, but it's a wasted emotion, I guess. Our father is dead.

Dead.

"Michael, hurry!" I shout but don't know if he can hear me.

Fear is a strobe light in my chest. The echo of a gunshot rings in my brain—a deafening bang that vibrates through my entire body.

Blood.

More blood.

The rain drives down in unrelenting sheets. My heart is pounding so hard I think I might pass out.

"I'm sorry, but your grandfather didn't make it."

"No!"

I scream the words, thrashing against the weight holding me down.

I can't breathe!

I can't breathe!

"No! Grandpa, no!"

"No!" I jolt up, breaths punching out of me as I wrestle free of the tangled sheets. My skin is slicked with sweat as the dream fades. But the feeling remains—a loud, pounding pain. A cry of agony resounding between my temples.

Closing my eyes, I fight for air, resting my elbows on my knees and supporting my head.

"Inhale," I whisper.

Forcing air through my nose, I hold it, letting it fill my lungs before slowly deflating.

I do this three more times before I can even start to think straight.

It was just a dream.

A memory.

Nausea sweeps through me as I fist my hair and will it away. I can't think about that night. I don't even know what triggered it.

Yes you do.

My eyes bulge, my head shooting up.

"Brody." I whisper my brother's name, reaching for my phone for an update.

It's been a harrowing forty-eight hours. I wish I could forget the dread that swept through me when I answered the phone two nights ago and listened to some guy named Azim shatter my world.

"Who are you?" I frowned, annoyed that I was talking to a stranger when the only person I really wanted to hear from was my twin brother. Brody hadn't called me back with an update on the whole Indigo situation, and I couldn't settle. I'd tried texting and calling, but I couldn't get through and had ended up reading late into the night to try and distract myself.

"Azim. I work for Castle Shaw. I'm essentially your brother's boss."

I scoffed. "Didn't you fire him this afternoon?"

He sighed, and that's when the dread seeped through me—a cold, sick warning. Bolting off my pillow, I flung my legs over the edge of my bed and demanded answers. "What's happened? Is Brody okay?"

"I'm sorry to tell you this, but he's been shot."

"Shot?" Rifle fire tore through my brain. Disbelief, shock, terror all fought for first place in my chest. Memories flooded me like a tidal wave, and I gasped for air. "What happened?"

"He was protecting…" Azim's voice trailed off as he obviously struggled to speak.

"Is he alive?"

"Yes, he's in surgery. I thought you'd want to be here when he wakes up."

If he wakes up.

I snapped my eyes closed, cursing my cynical brain as I pulled on clothes and hauled ass to the hospital.

It was the longest, worst night of my life. Or maybe second worst.

Whatever, it sucked.

And I'm still recovering.

My fingers shake as I text Brody's girlfriend.

. . .

Me: How's the big guy?

Indy: He's doing good. Ate some breakfast. Has been pretty alert all morning. Are you coming to see him today?

Me: Yeah. I'll just take a shower and get something to eat.

Indy: K. See you soon.

Relief floods me.

He's alive.

He made it.

He woke up.

I still have a brother. My only family. The one guy who's stuck with me, never let me down. I don't know what I'd do if I lost him. I can't even think about it.

Pacing the waiting room while we waited for him to get out of surgery was harrowing. Indy paced with me. Hugged me. Held my hand.

We were both wrecks, and when the doctor finally told us he was out of surgery and would be just fine, we dissolved into these blubbering tears. I hardly ever cry, but that was too much. I was a freaking mess. With Indy's little body tucked against mine, I laid my cheek on her head and we bawled together.

She's been an unexpected surprise in Brody's life. As

much as I hate the fact that she was the reason my twin got shot in the first place, I can tell how much Brody cares about her. So, I'm trying to do the right thing and be extra nice to her, look after her. She was so shaken up that night we first met. I could see her feelings for Brody right away, and they were totally genuine. I can't hold this shooting against her. It wasn't exactly her fault. It's not like she pulled a gun on herself.

Dark feelings brew as I think about the spoiled psycho who did pull the trigger. She better go down. She better—

My phone starts ringing, and I check the time.

Far out. I never sleep this late. Although, I'm kind of all over the place thanks to a few sleepless nights in the hospital. Grabbing my phone, I fling open the curtain above my bed and let the sunlight pour over the covers.

I read the name on my screen, and a smile curls my lips before I can stop it.

Nerves rocket through me as I press the green circle and answer, "Hey, Carmen. How's it going?"

"Hey, Jake." Her voice is so sweet. It's not high and breathy, just gentle with a slight husk to it. "I'm good. Sorry to call you on a Sunday."

"That's all right. I never mind hearing from you."

I cringe. Was that too much?

Pressing my lips together, I try to remind myself to play it cool. Carmen's with someone else; I shouldn't be in love with her. But she makes it impossible. I've liked her from the moment I met her last year. The first thing that captured me was her beauty. She's a Latina goddess with big brown eyes and a waterfall of thick, walnut-colored hair. We were placed in a study group together and hit it off immediately. That's when I spotted her dimples and she became so much more than just beautiful. Her smile could power a city. She's kind, intelligent, easy to talk to. She's just… everything.

I knew she had a boyfriend, so the idea of falling for her was a no-go. But we've spent so much time together, and we have so much in common. The big feels have grown without my say-so.

Carmen giggles. "You're sweet."

I scrub a hand down my face while my heart glows, the warmth shimmering through me and eradicating the nasty dream that woke me.

She always makes everything better.

I savor the sound of her voice as she asks me about my weekend.

Closing my eyes, I wonder if I should mention Brody, but it's so heavy and I don't want to worry her.

"Yeah, it's been eventful."

"That sounds intriguing."

I snicker but don't elaborate.

"You're all good, though, right?"

"Yeah." I nod. "Of course. Everything's good."

Which it is. Brody's alive. He's gonna make it. That is freaking good news, and I refuse to dwell on the fact that he could have died.

A shudder runs through me, but I force a brightness into my voice. "How about you? What have you been up to this weekend?"

"Not too much. Caught a movie on Friday night, then had to go to a concert with my mother last night."

"Oh, that band, right?"

Carmen laughs. "It's hardly a band. More like a classical string quartet. They're called *Cuerdas del Corazón*. It means heartstrings."

"Huh. That's clever. I like it."

"Yeah, I like the name too." The comment makes me grin. That's Carmen's sweet way of saying that's the only thing she likes about them.

"How painful was it?"

"You know me too well, Jake Adams."

I love that. I love that so freaking much.

Why aren't we together again?

"I did my daughter duty and won't complain. It meant the world to Mamá, so it was worth it."

She's got to be the nicest human on this planet.

I wish I could tell her that. I mean, I hint at it all the time, but I wish I could outright look her in the eye and tell her how I feel—*Carmen, you are the most amazing woman I know and I love you.*

"Anyway, the reason I'm calling is because Hector and I have hit a snag with this documentary trip. I'm over at his place now trying to figure it out."

And I'm brought back to reality.

Hector.

That's why I can't look her in the eye and tell her the truth.

Because of her boyfriend, Hector Cox.

Or Cockhead, as I like to refer to him in the privacy of my brain.

"Oh yeah?" I try to keep my voice light. "What kind of snag?"

"Well, the camera guy he lined up just bailed, and we need a new guy."

My heart kicks out of rhythm.

"It's proving to be a challenge since the trip is happening in like a couple of weeks. No one's available. But then I thought of you."

She thought of me.

"And I was wondering, since you're so good with that kind of thing, and I know you've got some gear…"

Is she asking me to come along, or does she just want to borrow the gear?

"I mean, I know it's probably inconvenient, but it'd just be like a long weekend in Minnesota. We're kind of testing the waters there because I have a contact who can help us. If the filming goes well, then Hector's hoping to hit up a bunch more national parks, make more than just a short film."

"Where in Minnesota?" I ask.

"Superior National Forest. It's about three hours north of Minneapolis. We can cover your travel expenses and—"

"You want me to be your camera guy?" My voice pitches with so much hope that I sound like an excited puppy. I cringe and clear my throat.

"Well, yeah. That'd be great. If you can, you'd kind of be saving our asses. This thing can't go ahead if we don't find a replacement and—"

"Yes." I answer before I can even think it through, but come on! Carmen is asking me to join her on a trip into a national forest where I get to spend a long weekend working right beside her. The entire long weekend!

"Oh really? That'd be so great! I knew you'd save the day." Her voice drops to a soft whisper. "Hector has been stressing out and ranting that the trip is ruined. I'm so relieved I can go inside and tell him it's not."

I close my eyes, wishing for the millionth time that I was her boyfriend and she was going inside to plan this trip with me.

But at least I'm coming along.

That's got to count for something, right?

She thought of me.

Because you're her friend with camera gear, you idiot! Nothing more.

But maybe this weekend is a chance to show her that I could be more. Or at least a chance to really gauge her relationship with Hector. They got together the summer after high school, but some of the comments she makes, and those little looks on her face when she thinks no one is watching... I can't help wondering how happy Hector really makes her.

This will be an opportunity for me to see them in a different setting.

Hector's a senior, and I only ever really see him when he strolls in to study group to pick her up or loiter around when he's got nothing better to do. He sits there, messing around on his phone and making stupid remarks while we're trying to get work done. It's frickin' annoying.

That's the only interaction I see between them. Other than that, I know what she's told me about him, and reading between the lines, I don't think she's in love.

Not the way I'm in love with her.

She deserves to be happy.

She deserves to be with a guy who will make her a top priority, treat her like she's important, worthwhile.

I don't think Hector does.

In fact, I think Hector is a lazy fool who has no idea how lucky he is.

"Thanks again, Jake. You are seriously the best."

"My pleasure. Really. I'm looking forward to it."

There's a soft pause, and then her honey voice makes my day all over again. "Me too."

I can hear how much she means it.

She's glad I'm coming along.

Yes!

"See you tomorrow."

"See ya," I whisper and hang up, dropping the phone on my rumpled bedsheets and lying back down, staring at the ceiling with a gooey smile until...

Shit.

Brody.

I sit up and swing my legs over the side of the bed. They dangle above my desk area as I grip the edge of the mattress.

Should I really be leaving him now?

He was shot.

Carmen said the trip is a couple weeks away. He should be better by then, right? And he's got Indy now.

But he was shot!

He nearly died, and I'm saying yes to taking off and leaving him. It's only for a long weekend, but still.

Jumping off the bed, I land on the wooden floor and rush to get ready.

I'll head to the hospital and casually run it by him now, throw it into the conversation and gauge his reaction from there. If he really doesn't want me to go, I won't.

Crossing my fingers, I race down to the dorm showers, keen to get this over with. I really can't let Carmen down, but Brody has been by my side since before we were born. I won't bail on him like everybody else has.

2

THE LIST CHECKER

Carmen

I CLASP the phone in my hand and cross my arms, gazing out over Mrs. Cox's beautiful garden. It's always been like this—serene with a redbrick pathway that meanders through the flowers. The early October weather is perfect today. The midday air is losing its crisp edge, promising a warm afternoon. The sky is blue, and the leaves are just thinking about changing color. It's my favorite time of year, the streets coming alive with golden hues.

And Jake said yes.

Relief pulses through me. Thank God I thought of him.

Now I can walk back into the house and tell Hector that his trip—his baby—is still going to come together. He can calm down, and I won't have to manage his fire anymore.

It's never a raging fire. Hector's not like that. But when he gets stressed out or pissed off, it's kind of exhausting. He gets snippety and sarcastic, his sentences coming out terse and short. Although, his rant about months of planning going down the toilet sure went on a while.

Pressing my lips together, I remember my role in this. I'm his support. The organizer. The list checker.

When he came up with the idea to make a short documentary last Christmas, he was pumped. So was his best friend, Lenny. He's the director on this project and has helped Hector write the script and decide how the short film will play out. It feels like every weekend has been taken up with this thing, and when I saw how disorganized they both were—they're dreamers, not doers—I asked if I could step in and help actually make this happen.

I've arranged the budget, the flights, the tour guide, the schedule. The only thing I wasn't in charge of was the cameraman, but I guess now that's on me too.

And thank goodness it's Jake.

A smile tugs at my lips as I think about my friend with his clear blue eyes and shy smile, his crop of floppy blond hair that always gets in his eyes but isn't long enough to tuck behind his ear. I don't know why he doesn't just cut it, but I'll never suggest that. I love his hair. I love the way he runs his fingers through it, or fists it when he's trying to concentrate, or plays with the short ends at the nape of his neck when he's nervous.

He's such a sweet guy, and I know I can rely on him not to let us down. We've been friends for just over a year, and in that time, he's always been a man of his word.

I'm so incredibly happy that he's joining us.

Pressing my hand against my jumping stomach, I remind myself not to be *that* happy. We're just friends. I'm with Hector.

It doesn't matter that Jake and I get along so well.

I'm with Hector.

And I have my reasons for that.

My lips purse as I turn away from the beautiful blooms and head back inside.

Lenny's bouncing a mini basketball on the floor and shooting for a hoop on the door while Hector lies on the couch, tapping his forehead with a pen.

The second he spots me, he jolts up and spears me with a questioning look.

"He said yes." I put my phone down on the coffee table and smile at my boyfriend.

"Good." He nods, matter-of-fact, like five minutes ago he wasn't cursing the sky.

I have to admit, I'm a little miffed by his reaction.

"Thank you, sweet Carmen, you've saved the day. What would I do without you?"

Would that be too much to ask?

"What's his name again?" Lenny shoots for the hoop and misses.

"Jake."

"And he's in your study group?"

"Yeah, we have a lot of classes together."

"Which one is he again?" Hector frowns at me.

I shoot him an incredulous look. "Jake. You see him all the time. When you pick me up, he's always there."

"Oh, wait, is he the weedy guy with the floppy hair? Kind of intense?"

"He's not... weedy." I frown. "And he's only intense because he's so smart."

"Yeah, I know the one." He nods, then gives me a sideways glance. "He is skinny, though, angel. You've got to admit that."

I shrug, not wanting to. So Jake is on the leaner side; that doesn't have to be a negative thing. Why does Hector have to be such a putz sometimes?

He clicks his fingers and points at my computer. "Anyway, last-minute details. Alejandro is all lined up, so what's left to finalize?"

I wake up the screen and check my meticulous list. I've got everything down to the contents of the first aid kit we'll be taking along. I don't want to miss a single thing.

Jotting down Jake's name next to "cameraman," I then run through the other details until finally Lenny stops missing the basketball hoop and looks to Hector with a grin.

"We're ready, man."

Hector smiles. "Yes we are."

"Time to make you the next David Attenborough."

They both start laughing, and I smile. Hector is a really good-looking guy. He may not have the suave British accent, but he's passionate about the environment, and he can be dynamic to watch.

If anyone can make a short film look good, it'll be him.

I'm glad I can be a part of this project, even if I'm not going to get much recognition for it. What we're doing is a good thing. Hector is all about highlighting the beauty of this planet, and his goal is to showcase rarely touched pockets of our natural environment and share it with the world, encouraging them to take care of our planet and preserve what we still can.

Alejandro was my next-door neighbor growing up... until he moved to Minnesota about ten years ago. We've kind of kept in touch, but I reached out when we were planning this trip, remembering that he was a park ranger at Superior National Forest. He left that job a while ago, but he still agreed to guide us around for a few days, taking us to the most stunning, remote places. It's going to be a fun adventure.

"Make sure you sort out a flight for Jake, and he'll need to get permission to get out of his classes that week."

I'm nodding, taking notes while Hector talks. I know all this already but don't want to make him feel bad, so I nod and type, adding in extra things he's not mentioning.

He turns to say something to Lenny, and I stare at Jake's name on my computer screen.

He sounded tired on the phone. At least I think he did. Maybe I'm reading too much into it, but something was off. I hope Jake's okay. Conversation with us tends to flow pretty smoothly, but he was being kind of cryptic about his weekend.

I can ask him about it again tomorrow.

It's interesting that Mondays have become my favorite day of the week.

They probably shouldn't be, but I get to sit next to Jake in two classes on a Monday, plus we have our afternoon study group together. It's not just me and him. It's never just me and him, but even getting to hang out in those crowded environments is fun. He's always passing me notes and saying things that make me smile.

He's so smart too.

And he listens. When I talk, he really listens.

I glance at Hector and swallow, feeling bad for thinking about Jake when I should probably be focusing on my boyfriend.

I wish I could break up with him.

The thought makes me flush. I glance down at my hands, noticing the slight tremble in my fingers. Gripping them together, I give my brain a sharp reprimand.

We've been through this before.

Breaking up with Hector is… it's a bad idea.

The fallout.

I bite the inside of my cheek. The weight that sometimes presses down on my chest, making it hard to breathe, is threatening to crush me. I steel myself against it.

Don't go there!

This isn't just about me… or Hector.

I can't hurt any more people. There's already been too much pain.

Hector's a good person. He's enough.

Closing my eyes, I force images of Jake to the back of

my mind and try to stay focused. I wouldn't even have doubts over Hector if I hadn't met Jake. It's just my brain playing tricks on me. So what if we get on great and have things in common? That doesn't mean I ditch my boyfriend. Jake probably doesn't even see me as more than a friend anyway. And that's what we are. Just friends. College buddies who will no doubt lose touch after we graduate.

My forehead wrinkles, and I push my finger between my eyebrows to smooth it out again.

You can't always get everything you want, and I have to be grateful for the things I do have. Like a boyfriend who saved me when I thought my world was ending.

3

NOT WHAT I WANT TO HEAR

Jake

I SPIN the keys around my index finger as I walk into the private hospital. The nurse behind the desk buzzes me through, and I walk down the corridor. This place is seriously fancy—shiny wood-laminate flooring, Brody's bathroom looks like it belongs in a luxury hotel, and the furniture in the room is stylish and modern. I've never even spent the night somewhere this nice… and it's a hospital!

I'm still kind of blown away that Castle Shaw is paying for all of Brody's care. I guess he owes my brother big-time for saving his daughter's life, but still… I'm not used to people doing nice things for us.

Brody and I have spent most of our lives fending for ourselves. There was that sweet reprieve at Grandpa Ray's where we tasted what a real childhood could look like, but then at fourteen, it got snatched away. Suddenly. In the most shocking way.

Then Cooper left.

It was a brutal blow, and followed so swiftly after Grandpa's death. I couldn't believe it. After that, social services split us up, put Deeks and Michael into a group home and sent Brody and me to a foster family.

They were nice. I liked them.

But then they moved out of state and didn't want to take us with them. It was just after Deeks and Michael took off.

Yeah, our brothers left us. Ran away one night. Forgot all about the fact that we still needed them.

Anger burns, sharp and bright.

I rub my stomach, trying to get back to that happy mindset I was in. The one where I was grateful for Castle Shaw's generosity and internally happy-dancing that Carmen's invited me on this epic trip.

I better unearth my camera gear and make sure it's still working. I bought it off Craigslist for a steal. The guy was moving overseas and selling up. Everything he'd bought on a whim, he was getting rid of. And I scored big.

I felt pretty damn cool turning up for the group project we were working on and rather than having to film it with our phones and tablets, I was able to produce professional-quality gear and make us look awesome.

We aced that assignment.

My lips toy with a smile as I hear Carmen's excited laughter in my head.

"Ahhh! We were the best!"

I gave her a sideways hug, resisting the urge to sniff her luscious hair, and joined the rest of our group in celebrating at Peter's Pantry—a local diner that made the best thick shakes and served the kind of food Aunt Nell used to make. Good ol' fashioned chow that smelled delicious and tasted even better.

Slowing to a stop, I lightly knock on Brody's door and let myself in.

The first thing I see is Indigo curled up beside my brother. She looks so tiny beside him, yet she seems to fit like a puzzle piece.

How can I not be happy for my little bro?

"Hey, guys." I grin, lifting my hand in a wave before shoving it into my pocket.

How do I start this thing?

So, Bro, I know you're shot and everything, but I want to take off to Minnesota for a little bit. You cool with that?

I internally cringe and get to work on a better speech while my big little brother greets me. That's our standard joke. I was born first, but he's always been bigger than me. In that way, we're both each other's big brother... and little brother.

A smile curls my lips just thinking about it. Mom thought it was the funniest thing. Even though she died when I was only six, I still remember her laughing over that one. She had a great laugh.

"Hey." Brody's voice is croaky, his eyes taking me in with a look of uncertainty.

I immediately tense. I know that look. Something's off.

What's going on?

My stomach tightens, but I try to play it cool. Whatever he has to say can't ruffle me. Not when he's recovering from a gunshot wound. No matter what he says, I refuse to argue with him. So, I'll start by just pretending that I can't see that look on his face.

Lightly laying my hand on his covered foot, I force a smile. "How you feeling?"

Brody stares me down for a long moment, and my stomach's actually starting to hurt when he softly says, "Jake... we gotta talk."

I run a hand through my hair and try to make light of it. "Sounds ominous. Better lay it on me quickly."

Brody sighs, and I hate that sound so freaking much.

"Deeks and Michael were here."

I flinch. I can't help it.

What?

That can't be right. Two names I never thought I'd hear again. Two people I never thought I'd see again. They're here? They... "What?"

"They heard about what happened on the news. They've been looking for us."

"Oh really?" My scathing tone is pretty caustic, but I couldn't stop it if I tried.

They've been looking for us. As if!

They took off.

They ran away, never thought to take us with them, just left. No note. No goodbye. No nothing.

They're not interested in Brody and me; they proved that years ago!

I can't help a little scoff. "Looking for us?"

"Yeah, that's what they said." Brody sniffs, the right side of his mouth curling into a smile. "It was so good to see them again. You should hear what they've been through and what they're—"

"I don't want to hear it," I snap, this weird sensation buzzing in my throat. It's tight and uncomfortable. I don't want to think about my brothers. I'm over it. "I don't need some shitty-ass explanation," I spit. "They left us. Just took off. They didn't even leave a frickin' note! As far as I'm concerned, I only have one brother. That's you." I point at Brody, hating the sad look on his face right now.

"Jay, come on, man. You don't know their stories. They were scared kids."

"And we weren't?" I slap my chest. "We needed them, and they left us!"

"They didn't know our foster home was going to fall through."

"It doesn't matter! They abandoned us, just like Cooper did!"

My voice is rising, words spewing out of my mouth in hot chunks. I never yell. It feels so out of place for me. And I said I wasn't going to get mad with Brody. He's recovering.

I need to calm the hell down.

But I can't.

There's a thunderstorm in my chest. My throat hurts.

I lightly touch it, wishing I could scratch away this sensation. Why do I feel like crying?

I'm not crying! Deeks and Michael don't deserve my tears.

"Is everything okay in here?" Two nurses appear in the doorway. The older one gives Indy a reprimanding look.

"Yeah, we're good." Brody raises his hand, looking weak and pale.

Indy carefully slips off the bed, flashing a contrite smile before flicking her gaze to me.

I glance at the nurses.

"You need to stop that yelling. People are here to rest and recover."

"Yes, ma'am." I nod, attempt a smile, then turn back to Brody as they walk away.

He's looking at me like he's trying to read my mind. I hate it when he does that, but I can't turn my head away. How do I make him understand?

We don't want Deeks and Michael back in our lives. They'll only hurt us again. How can he trust so easily? How can he just welcome them back in?

"They really want to see you," he rasps.

"Well, they're fresh out of luck."

My comment hurts Brody, but I can't take it back.

I'm not opening myself up to that bullshit right now.

I'm finally enjoying life. I go to a great school. I'm acing all my classes. I own a car—it's a piece of crap, but it's still mine. For the first time ever, I'm in control, and I don't want to do anything to screw it up.

Crossing my arms, I grip my shirtsleeves and change the subject. "I spoke to Carmen this morning. Their camera guy's bailed on this trip they've been organizing. It's filming a short documentary in a national forest in Minnesota. She's invited me to go instead."

Brody's eyebrows slowly rise, and he starts nodding. It's obvious he's let down by my subject change, but he's a good enough guy to appreciate what I'm saying.

Carmen has invited me to go along!

This is huge!

"If you're good, then I'm gonna go, but..." My eyes skirt the room, hating this awkward tension between us. Brody's my man. He has been my entire life. I don't want this to come between us. "But if you need me, I'll stay."

"No, man, you should go. This is a great opportunity. And it's Carmen, right?" He wiggles his eyebrows, and I'm quickly reassured that nothing could ever really come between us.

I laugh and have to admit, "Her boyfriend's gonna be there. Unfortunately. This project is his baby. The guy wants to be the next David Attenborough."

Brody snickers. "Well, this could be your perfect chance to prove you're the better man."

Oh, I wish!

I smile, but know it's a pipe dream. I have grand ideas of telling Carmen how I really feel, but can I honestly do it?

She's obviously with Hector for a reason. Maybe if I could find out what it is, that'll help me let her go. Move on. I don't know.

"I guess I'll see you when you get back?" Brody's voice sounds small and tentative. It's so unlike him.

"Yep." I nod, wanting to run over and hug him.

Of course you'll see me when I get back!

But... "Where are you gonna be?"

Brody's swallow is thick, and my insides start caving in.

"I don't know yet."

That is so not the answer I want to hear. Is Brody going to see Michael and Deeks again? Have they invited him to come and live with them or something?

I don't want to know.

I can't hear this right now.

I try to smile, act like this isn't killing me. Brody's a grown man. He's always come to me for help, kept me in his circle, but there's something in his eyes right now. He's holding back the truth, because he knows I won't approve.

I should call him on it, but I won't.

Because I can't deal right now.

Walking around the bed, I hold out my fist. "I'll call you."

Brody bumps his fist against mine. "You better."

I gaze at him for a moment, then turn and leave before anything more can be said.

I don't want to yell at him. I don't want to try and explain myself when I can see the hurt on his face.

He's wounded.

He needs to heal. Recover.

He believes Michael and Deeks won't hurt us again.

What do I do?

Try to convince him he's wrong?

Or maybe he just has to learn the hard way.

I'll be there to pick up the pieces when Michael and Deeks ditch him again. I swore I'd never do that to Brody, and I won't. Even when we don't agree about everything, I'm with him until the end.

With shaking fingers, I rub my mouth, storming out of the hospital and trying not to look at anybody. My insides are writhing.

Deeks.

Michael.

They're in LA.

They want to see me.

Slamming into my car, I grip the wheel and remind myself that I don't want to see them.

Some things you can forgive. And then there's that stuff that's so big, so huge, so painful that you just have to shut it down. There's no room for forgiveness. For any kind of emotion.

Sometimes it's better not to feel anything.

4

SCRAMBLED EGGS WITH A SIDE OF DEBATE

Carmen

I RUN a brush through my hair, checking my reflection and the light application of makeup. Leaning forward, I brush a finger beneath my eyes, loving the chocolate shade of eye shadow I bought last week. The earthy tones suit my skin and really make my eyes pop.

With a satisfied nod, I head downstairs, the smell of Huevos pericos igniting my taste buds. Scrambled eggs with tomato and onion are a favorite of my father's, and Mamá knows it. I'd usually sit down for some too, but I'm running late. It's not like me to sleep in, but I was tossing and turning last night, struggling to switch my brain off. It ran from the safety of a checklist to the unsettling complication of what to do about Hector.

Schooling my features, I make sure none of my uncertainty is showing as I glide into the kitchen.

"*Buenos días*," I greet my parents, stepping around the table and giving Papá a kiss on the cheek.

He flicks his newspaper, winking at me—a silent good morning greeting.

"*¿Dormiste bien?*" my mother asks me as I peck her made-up cheek.

She always looks perfect. Makeup applied with precision and care, her nails beautifully manicured, her outfit preplanned the night before.

With a little humph, she answers the question I haven't responded to yet with her own answer. "I slept okay, once I eventually got to sleep. You were home late last night." Her dark eyebrow arches, and I try to ignore the fact that she's slipped into English. Oh, and that I'm nineteen years old and no longer have a curfew. I'm a sophomore in college, for crying out loud. I technically could be living in a dorm, away from home with no parent lying awake and wondering when I'll be walking in the door.

I could be completely free.

Except I can't.

I have to stay.

Licking my lips, I reply in kind. "We were finalizing details for the trip."

Mamá's shoulders tense. They do that every time I mention Minnesota.

Not wanting to get caught in another debate, I quickly surge forward with the facts. "The cameraman can't do it anymore, so we had to find a new one. Jake Adams is coming instead."

"Jake Adams," Papá murmurs, like he's trying to place the name.

I turn to face him, preferring his thoughtful look to the sharp eye my mother is giving me. "He's in my study group. We have a few classes together."

He still looks blank.

"He started the same time as me last year."

Papá shakes his head, and I give up with an eye roll, quickly opening the pantry.

"*Deberías tomar un desayuno adecuado,*" Mamá pipes up above the sizzling, lifting the pan and scraping eggs onto Papá's plate.

"I don't have time to sit down for breakfast." I shove a granola bar in my bag and start preparing a coffee to go.

"*No me agrada esto.*" Mamá places the plate in front of Papá, then spins with her hand on her hip.

The coffee machine starts whirring, and I rest my hands on the counter with a sigh.

Of course my mother wouldn't let the chance for debate slip through her fingers.

She flicks her pretty red nails at me and starts off with the same question she always does. "Are you sure this trip is a good idea?"

I check my watch, my insides jittering. Hector will be here to pick me up any moment. We drive to school together most days. I have my own car, but he likes to take me, and Papá prefers it that way. For some reason, he thinks it's safer. It drives me crazy, but I can't argue with him. I have enough on my plate arguing with Mamá every day.

If she had her way, I'd never leave the freaking house.

I mean, sure, they're proud of me that I'm acing it at Stanford, but ever since—

Snapping my eyes shut, I cut off the thought before it can bloom.

Clenching my jaw, I quickly mutter, *"No otra vez con lo mismo. Por favor, Mamá."*

"Yes, this again. Of course this again! You're flying halfway across the country to hike through some isolated woods. What about wild animals! Slips! Falls! Bad weather!"

I sniff in a slow breath, trying to calm myself and speak softly. "Alejandro is going to be our guide. The reason we're going to that park is so he can be there to help us." I'm speaking slowly, desperate for her to understand. "You don't trust him? He spent almost every afternoon here when we were kids."

"Of course I trust him," she clips, her chin trembling as she opens the cupboard and pulls out a Tupperware container. As she shovels in a healthy amount of eggs, I watch the steam curl over the sides before she clips the lid on and hands it to me. "You can eat in the car."

I stare at the food, tempted to ignore it, but my mother has never been good at taking no for an answer. And now her bottom lip is trembling.

Grabbing a fork from the drawer, I slam it shut and snatch the container out of her hands. *"Gracias,"* I mutter.

Her reprimanding frown eases as I use my manners, but then she's at me again, speaking in a flurry of Spanish.

I shouldn't be going.

It's too far away.

It's not my project.

I'll be missing classes.

"I got permission from every one of my professors! It's only five nights away. Alejandro will be there the entire time, just like you insisted. I don't know what more you want from me!"

"Does Hector really need you to go?"

"He wants me there. I'm his assistant and in charge of logistics. I'm the glue holding this entire project together. I can't just bail on him because you don't want me to go."

"Diego, help me out!" Mamá gestures to her husband, who is now hunched over his eggs.

Sitting back, he wipes his chin with a napkin and shrugs. "As long as Hector's there to look after her, I think she should go."

My eyes are tempted to start rolling again, but then Mamá's hands go up in surrender, and the silence is blessed peace.

I bask in it for just a moment before the front door opens and Hector strolls in.

"Good morning, Díaz family." He grins and Mamá lets out a gushing sound, swiftly walking around me to hug him.

She murmurs something in Spanish about how handsome he is and how lucky we are to have him.

He doesn't speak that much Spanish, but I think he picked up the handsome part.

He throws me a proud wink before kissing my mother on each cheek.

She hugs him again. "Oh, have you had breakfast?"

"Yes. I had my standard protein shake."

"Good, healthy boy." She pats his flat stomach with a laugh and wanders back into the kitchen to start rinsing out the fry pan.

I look to my father, hitching my bag onto my shoulder as he rises from the table to kiss my cheek.

"You go have your adventure. Don't you worry about Mamá. I'll look after her."

"Gracias, Papá. Te amo."

He pulls me into a tight hug and calls over my shoulder. "Hector, you'll look after my baby girl, right?"

"Of course, sir. I always look after her."

I pull out of my father's embrace to catch the grin between them. They act like they're father and son.

But they're not.

Glancing down to the empty chair at the end of the table, I imagine another man sitting there. The one who died too soon and left a gaping hole in all our lives.

Hector filled it a little. He sits in that chair when he comes over for dinner now. I've never liked it, but I can't tell anyone that because it feels petty and immature.

Watching my mother smile at Hector, at the quiet

looks he shares with my father... he's become a part of this family. My parents love him.

Can I honestly put an end to that?

They'll never understand.

They think he's perfect.

And if I break up with him, that chair at the end of the table will be empty all over again. The house might go back to that deafening silence that nearly killed us all... to that dread that wafted through the house as we all tried to come to terms with the fact that my big brother would never be coming home, never be sharing a meal with us ever again.

5

UNEXPECTED VISITORS

"WELL, THAT'S GOOD NEWS." Marty, from my study group, lightly slaps my shoulder, and I nod in agreement.

"Yeah. It's great." I try for a smile, but it feels half-hearted.

I should be stoked. All of my professors have agreed to give me time off to go to Minnesota. Every one of them said it'll be a great experience and I can catch up when I get back. That'll mean more study time with Carmen.

Plus, plus, plus.

Tick, tick, tick.

But I still feel like shit.

Thanks to Brody.

He called me while I was eating lunch. Texted first, asked to talk. I didn't want to call him back, knowing it was going to be awkward. I guessed what he was going to say before he even said it.

"Indy and I are going to head to the ranch for a while. It'll be a chance to get her away from the media, and it's as good a place as any to heal."

I slumped forward on the concrete bench seat, staring at the ground, my heart thrumming so hard I could barely hear myself speak. I felt like I'd just been punched in the stomach. "The ranch?"

"Yeah, Deeks and Michael are doing it up. They've fixed the house and they're buying cattle, turning it into a working ranch again."

The air in my lungs felt like nettles—stinging, burning. "The ranch. In Montana."

"Yeah."

It was impossible to talk after that. So I just sat and listened, not giving anything away as I flicked those switches inside me and made sure the emotions stayed in check.

Don't feel.

Be numb.

Stay calm, unemotional.

I remind myself of that as I wave goodbye to my classmate and head back to my dorm.

"Don't feel," I mutter under my breath, trying not to be pissed off or... whatever the hell I am.

The ranch.

Grandpa's ranch.

They're bringing it back to life.

But how are they going to do that when he's not there?

He was the heartbeat of that place. I don't know if I can ever go back there. It'll feel so empty and cold without him.

Scratching my neck, I swallow past the lump in my throat. It hurts to swallow, but of course it's all I seem to be able to do as I ram that emotion back where it belongs.

"Don't feel," I snap, shoving my hands in my jacket pockets and picking up my pace.

I just want to get inside, have some snacks, and dive into my latest assignment. That'll distract me.

That'll—

I jerk to a stop when I spot two guys loitering outside my building.

I recognize them immediately. Sure, they're older, but it's still them. Still Deeks and Michael.

My brothers.

An ache blooms in my chest—this weird kind of yearning. It makes my eyes sting, and I blink rapidly, wondering if I should turn away before they spot me.

But I'm too late.

Deeks's face lights with a wide grin, and he raises his hand in the air and starts waving it.

"Jake!" He sprints across the street, and I've got nowhere to go. "Hey, man."

I glance at him, then look past his shoulder. Michael's walking slowly toward us, his hands in his jacket pockets, a resigned smile on his face.

He can read me better than Deeks can.

Or maybe Deeks is just choosing to ignore the expression on my face.

When I don't say anything, his smile falters, his lips pursing to the side while I silently curse Brody for selling me out. *What the shit?* I can't believe he told them where I was when I specifically said I didn't want to see them!

We're soon a huddle of three, sharing these awkward stares—a mixture of angst and confusion.

A couple wanders past us, the girl glancing over her shoulder like she can feel the tension.

"What are you guys doing here?" I finally mutter.

Deeks starts smiling again. "Had to see you."

"I told Brody I wasn't interested in reconnecting."

"We know. We ignored him." Deeks shrugged.

Michael's still staring at me, kind of misty-eyed. He looks like Brody a little, whereas Deeks looks more like me—the fine, sharp facial features, the leaner build, the angular jaw. I rub mine and look to the ground, not wanting to study them.

They look older, but in a different way. Like they've seen more than their fair share.

Brody said I had no idea what they've been through.

But... I can't!

The last time we got together as a family, they never said a freaking thing about splitting.

I stared at Michael's fat lip, threading my fingers together and wishing I had the right words to say. The bruise on his chin looked kind of nasty. He was obviously having a hard time at school. Or maybe it was the group home. Glancing at Deeks's red knuckles, I was reassured that at least someone was standing up for Michael. That was what Brody did for me.

We were family. We looked out for each other, just the way Grandpa taught us to.

Cooper obviously missed that lesson or he'd be with us. Looking after us so we didn't have to be split up and torn apart.

"What did the principal say?" Brody asks.

Deeks shrugged. "It was my final strike. I'm out. Lady who runs the group home is pretty pissed, but she'll look for another school." Leaning back with a huff, he crossed his arms. "Waste of freaking time. I don't want go to school anymore anyway."

Michael fingered the split on his lip and didn't say anything.

I wondered if it hurt him to talk. I wanted to ask, but then that'd force him to talk, so I kept the question to myself.

Instead I sat there quietly, wishing Grandpa would miraculously come back to life, that he'd stroll into the room and whisk us back to the ranch.

"Group home sucks too," Deeks kept muttering, then kicked me lightly under the table. "How's foster care?"

I shrugged. "Our family's pretty nice."

"Yeah, they're cool." Brody nodded. "Graham plays basketball. They've got a hoop out front. Donna's a pretty good cook, and she's nice. Her jokes are kind of lame, though."

The edge of Deeks's mouth tipped up, and Michael tried to smile but then winced and started dabbing his lip again.

"You guys got lucky." Deeks nodded. "Glad you're with someone good."

A fat silence fell on the table between us. We couldn't seem to breach it as we all got lost in our own thoughts. I wondered if they were thinking about Cooper like I was. How he took off without a goodbye. How it was coming up on a year since losing Grandpa, yet the pain felt as fresh as the day before.

"So, you guys are doing good," Michael whispered, his head bobbing up and down.

"Yeah." I tried to lift my voice, make it sound brighter. He looked like he needed the reassurance, so I gave it to him. "I'm liking school. I'm learning some awesome stuff." I wanted to say, *More than Grandpa could teach me*, but I didn't dare. I never wanted to sound as though I'd rather be there than with him at the ranch. But the learning was my salvation. It was the only thing getting me out of bed in the morning.

"I've joined a football team," Brody offered. "They said I'm good."

Deeks nodded. "You'd be awesome at that."

"Yeah, it's fun." Brody tried for a smile, and I bet he wanted to tell the story about how he sacked the quarterback in his first practice.

But he didn't.

And the silence came back. It was an awful disjointed

wait as our allocated time puttered to an end and our caseworkers rounded us back up.

"See you guys in a couple weeks." Brody waved, clueless to my brothers' intentions.

We went our separate ways that day.

And we never saw them again.

Until now.

Shit. Had they known that was the last time they'd see us?

Anger bubbles and boils over, a wretched tug in my gut that makes me snap. "Look, I didn't ask you to come here. Just... get lost. I've got shit to get done."

"Come on, Jake." Michael finally speaks. His voice is deeper, and it takes me off guard. I stand still, staring at the man he's become. "Please give us a chance to explain."

"Explain what? How you took off with no warning? How you just left us without a goodbye?"

"We didn't know your foster family was going to move only a few months later," Deeks murmurs.

"That's got nothing to do with it!" I fling my arm up. "We were a *family*, and I don't care how shitty things got, you don't just abandon the people you love! Grandpa was dead. Cooper was gone. You were all we had left, and you just took off!"

Deeks scrubs a hand down the back of his head. "We didn't mean to hurt you."

"Yeah, well, it doesn't hurt anymore!" The words are out before I've even thought about them.

Michael's expression drops like I've punched him in the face.

Deeks's forehead dents with a frown.

I lower my voice, going for cool and detached. That's the only way I'll get through this.

"I've learned to live without you. I don't need you in my life."

Deeks huffs and shakes his head. "We want to be part of your life again. We want you to come back to the ranch."

"Even just to visit." Michael steps forward, his blue eyes so hopeful. So deluded. "It's time to bring you home, man."

"I am home." I point to the student housing. "I don't need you guys. Brody's my family, and that's enough."

"He's coming back with us."

"I know that!" I snap. "But he's the only brother who's never let me down. He might be going to the ranch, but I trust him to keep in touch, to visit, to make me part of his life."

"We want that too."

"Yet I don't trust you." I eye them both, my gaze no doubt as sharp as my tone. "You made it clear that you didn't need family. Why the hell should that change now?"

"Please, Jake—"

"Leave me alone." I flick Deeks away when he tries to

reach for me. Holding up my hand, I step back like they're predators I'm trying to escape. My finger shakes when I point it between them. "I mean it. You fucking leave me alone."

I step off the curb and sprint across the street. Fumbling with my keycard, I have to swipe it twice before I'm able to wrench the door open. I escape inside, not looking back, knowing they're probably still standing there watching me leave. By the time I reach my room, I'm out of breath and fighting these weird puffs that sound more like sobs.

Resting my hands on my hips, I lean against my door and suck air in through my nostrils.

It's over.

It's done.

I said my piece, and now I need to stop thinking about it.

My bag slips off my shoulder, and I catch it before my laptop can hit the floor. Resting it gently by my bed, I pace to the window, tempted to look out of it, but I stop myself in the nick of time.

I don't want to see them.

I don't want to see them waiting or walking away.

None of it.

The phone in my back pocket starts to ring. I know who it is before I snatch it out and decline Brody's call.

He'll hate that, but I can't talk right now.

I'll say something mean, and he's been shot. I'm too pissed to talk to him and not make him feel bad. Even though he kind of deserves it.

The phone rings a second time, and I press the X again, then text my brother.

Not now. Just let me process.

Brody sends back a thumbs-up.
Here when you need me.

I toss the phone on my desk, knowing that's true. Brody has proven it time and time again. He's always been there. Always showed up when I needed him. He fought back the bullies, he did extra chores so I could study, he helped me relocate to Stanford even when I knew he was gutted I was moving away. He was proud of me for graduating with honors, for getting the scholarship. He's been my biggest cheerleader, my most loyal fan.

And now he's going to Montana.

Resting my hands on the back of my chair, I grip the wood and close my eyes.

Please, don't let them hurt Brody.

They probably won't. He bounces back pretty damn fast. He's got that knack of letting go, is one of those guys who can brush things off and look on the bright side. Life's simpler for a person like Brody.

Sometimes I wish I were more like him.

"But I'm me," I murmur, hearing Grandpa's voice in my head.

"You be you, son. You be the best you you can possibly be." He'd always grin and wink at me after saying something like that.

He understood. He got the fact that I was the runt of the litter. Physically I could never keep up with my brothers, but mentally I was ahead of them all. Grandpa called it my superpower. He never made me feel bad for being the weakling.

"You be you," I whispered, aching for a little more time with him. "You be you."

My eyes pop open, and I snatch a pen and paper off my desk. I need to think about something else, focus on something logical, unemotional.

I need to be me.

With a shaking hand, I pull out my chair and sit down to start making a list of all the things I'll need for the upcoming trip. As the sun sinks below the horizon, I absorb myself in preparation, pulling out my camera gear and checking it over, and then unearthing my pack and survival gear. Might as well be prepared.

You never know what a trip like this could throw at you, and I like being the guy with the first aid kit, the compass, and the flashlight.

I was always the most prepared person on the ranch, and I've taken that with me into life.

This trip couldn't come at a better time.

I need it.

Something to focus on, pour my energy into.

I'll be the most prepared guy in the group. The one

Carmen can turn to if anything goes wrong. That's the role I like to play, and I'm going to freaking ace it.

I have to.

I need to get away from here for a bit, find my calm again.

Balling my fingers into a fist, I flick them out and attempt to add a couple more things to my list.

6

HIGH EXPECTATIONS

Carmen

THE LAST TWO weeks have disappeared in a flurry of activity. Cramming in study and preparation, reassuring my parents that I'm going to be okay, and dealing with a slightly stressed-out Hector and a slightly sullen Jake has been all-consuming.

I frown, wondering how Jake will be when he comes out with all his stuff. We're parked outside his building, waiting for him to come down.

Crossing my arms, I try not to worry about the fact that we've been a little disjointed. Conversation hasn't flowed as per usual, and I don't know why. We've been surrounded by people the entire time, so I haven't really had the chance (or the courage) to ask what's wrong.

Maybe I will this weekend.

Wow. This weekend.

I can't believe we're loading up for the trip. That it's actually happening.

I'm here.

I'm doing it.

Saying goodbye to my mother this morning was a bit of a mission. She wouldn't let me go, clung to my shoulders like I was disappearing off to war.

Not me.

That was my brother's role.

An image of him standing tall and proud in his army fatigues slaps me in the face.

I blink and pull myself into line. Ademir, with his broad smile, so like mine. I can still see him so clearly.

"Can't believe you're a soldier now." I stared at the uniform hanging over the back of his chair and shook my head.

He laughed, continuing to pack his things. It was his last night before he shipped out, and I was trying to spend every spare second with him.

Sitting cross-legged on his bed, I watched him neatly fill his regulation bag.

"I always loved G. I. Joe."

I wrinkled my nose at him.

"What?" He laughed. "It'll be an adventure."

"I just want you to be safe," I finally admitted. "I want you to come home again."

"Hey." He stopped packing, crouching down so he could look me in the eye. "I'm gonna be fine. I promise I'll come back."

I tried to smile, but my lips just twitched and sank into a sad pout. I'd missed him so much while he was away at basic training. I liked having my brother around. He wasn't just family, he was my best friend.

"Stop that sad face." He pointed at me. "I'm strong, remember? I'm fast. I'm fire."

He struck out with a playful punch that I countered, just the way he'd taught me to.

"Oooo, girl's got skills."

He tried to come at me again and we ended up tussling, our laughter growing out of control until Mamá flung open the door and rained down a flurry of Spanish on us.

We're too noisy. We'll disturb the whole street. Let Ademir pack in peace!

She spun away, and we gave each other impish grins. I winced, hating being told off.

"Don't worry, *hermana*. She's all bark and no bite."

I sat up with a glum smile. "She's more barky than usual. She doesn't want you to go either."

"Only because I'm so awesome." He wriggled his eyebrows at me, and I had to laugh.

But then my smile faded away and I grabbed his wrist before he could continue packing. "You are awesome. You're the best person I know."

"Aw. I love you too." He winked at me, and my heart simultaneously bloomed and broke.

He never kept his promise.

He didn't come back.

And life's not the same without him.

"I'm here." Jake walks out of his building, bags on his shoulders and clutched in his hands. He looks like a bellboy. "Sorry for being a couple minutes late."

Catching his eye, I give him a little smile, and he responds in kind.

Phew. That's good. Smiling's good.

My grin grows until I notice the curve of his bicep as he hauls the heavy bags into the back of Hector's car. Jake's not weedy. He might be on the lean side, but he's strong. He told me once that he likes to rock climb for fun, and I can absolutely see that in him.

I bet he looks gorgeous when he's climbing—smooth, elegant moves as he works his way up a wall or rock face.

My eyes track him as he closes the trunk and wipes his hands on the back of his cargo pants. Tugging his T-shirt down, he comes to stand beside me while Hector finishes up his phone call.

Oh my gosh, Jake smells so good. Whatever deodorant he's wearing tickles my taste buds, and I have to spin away, making a beeline for the front seat so I'll be farther away from him.

This isn't good.

Maybe inviting him on this trip is a really bad idea. It's

like someone putting a chocolate bar on my plate and telling me I can't eat it.

Jake approaches my open window, loitering by the car while I buckle up. The pensive look on his face makes me study him. He's been quiet the last couple weeks. Ever since I invited him to come, actually.

Oh crap, did he not want me to? Did he just say yes because he's a nice guy who never wants to let anyone down?

Not that I can really do anything about that now. We're leaving for the airport in five minutes!

But still. I don't want this trip to be full of tension. It's supposed to be this fun experience. Glancing over my shoulder, I notice Hector still intent on his phone call and take the chance to quietly ask Jake how he's doing.

"Are you okay?" I murmur, running a hand down my long braid.

Jake nods, watching my movements before flashing me a tight smile. "I'm fine."

"Are you sure? Because—"

"Yep. I'm sure."

He nods once and walks around to the other side of the car, slipping in beside Lenny.

I watch him buckle up, but he avoids my gaze. Dammit. This is awful. I really want to find out what's going on, but Lenny's right there, and Jake's a private person.

But he usually talks to me.

I worry my lip, wondering what I can say to smooth things over. I've been so looking forward to getting to spend some extra time with Jake. This will be the first time we've hung out without assignments and projects hanging over our heads. I mean, yeah, we'll still have work to do, but we won't be in a library or a study hall. We're going to be in a remote forest. It'll be amazing. I can't wait to see him in that environment. I can't wait to see *myself* in that—

My phone starts ringing. I snatch it up, embarrassed that I have the volume so loud.

"*Hola, Mamá.*"

"*Hola, mi niñita.*" Mamá's voice is quavering, and I close my eyes, keeping the call in Spanish as I explain to her once again that I'll be safe. I'll come home in one piece.

I want to tell her that I'm not being deployed, that there are no bombs or ambushes waiting for me. But that will just remind her of how we lost Ademir, and she's worried enough as it is.

I promise to call her when the plane lands, and again at the ranger's station, before softly reminding her that I'll be out of cell phone range for a few days, but I'll still be safe.

"*Créeme. No haré nada tonto.*" I promise to look after myself.

She lets out a soft chuckle, grateful Hector is there to take care of me.

I roll my eyes but "Hmm" appropriately. It's what she needs to hear.

"*Nos vemos en seis diás.*"

"*Sí, Mamá.*"

Six days. It'll be the longest I've ever been away from home.

I hope she can handle it.

I hope I can too.

Giving my chest a little rub, I choose "See ya later" instead of goodbye and hang up.

Placing my phone in the console between the seats, I glance into the back and notice Jake's eyes on me. His smile gives me the impression he understood most of my phone call.

My forehead wrinkles, and he just gives me a soft grin.

"My mother," I explain anyway. "She worries."

"She cares."

My lips part. "Did you understand that call?"

"Some of it."

"When did you learn to speak Spanish?"

"Foster care number six, I think." His expression scrunches, his eyes darting to Lenny.

But Lenny's got his buds in and his head is already bobbing to music. I can faintly hear it blasting into his ears.

I press my lips together, desperately hoping for more, but all I get is a quiet "They were from Chile." He shrugs. "And I can't speak fluently, but I can pick up some things. I took it at school. I should probably speak it better, but I've got no one to practice with."

"Me." I point to myself. "You could have been practicing with me."

He snickers. "I didn't know you spoke it so well."

I slump back in my seat, facing the front and realizing that maybe Jake and I don't talk as much as I thought.

But we do.

We just don't always talk about the stuff from our past. Like the fact that Jake was in more than a few foster homes. Number six. Yikes. Poor guy. I knew he and Brody were orphans, but he's never really talked about how his parents died or how long he was in foster care.

Must have been a while.

"It's nice that your mom cares."

His soft voice surprises me, and I look into the back seat again. "Yeah. I guess. Sometimes it feels kind of smothering."

"I get that, but at least she gives a shit, you know?"

He looks out the window, gripping the handle above him and obviously wanting this conversation to end.

I understand.

I know what it's like to lose someone you love, and I never want to talk about it.

Spinning the ring on my middle finger, I let the silence reign while we wait for Hector.

I wish we could get back to the easy banter we usually have going, and now my worries are starting to compound.

Jake doesn't want to be here.

So he'll politely just suffer it for my sake. For Hector.

This is so not the way I wanted it to be.

But who am I kidding?

What? Did I expect to be next to him in the back seat,

laughing and joking around while my boyfriend drove us to the airport?

Things can't be that way, so maybe this is better.

This trip isn't even about me.

It's about Hector and what he needs.

I'm doing this for him.

And then I'll come home for Mamá and Papá. I'll continue to be the good girl who makes sure everyone is happy and not hurt. Who keeps herself together, because if she lets it show too much or for too long, she might lose it.

Nerves scatter through me as Hector slips into the car and we take off to the airport.

This is it. The moment I've been so looking forward to.

It's kind of sad that I have this awful feeling my expectations are way too high.

7

A FLIGHT TO REMEMBER

THE MUTED SOUND of the plane engine outside the window lulls me into a stupor. It's my first time on an airplane. Not that I told anyone that. I didn't want to embarrass myself in front of people who have no doubt flown all over the world.

Hector's rich, that's easy to see.

I think Carmen's from money too. There's a classy elegance about her, but it's tempered by her beautiful humility.

Shit, I was horrible to her in the car.

I should have been more friendly. More open.

But it just kind of dawned on me as I watched Hector

packing up the car. He's going to be with us the whole freaking time. This isn't going to be an amazing time away with Carmen. It's going to be time away with Carmen and her boyfriend.

I mean, I guess I kind of knew that, but it didn't really sink in because I haven't had time to dwell on it. I've been too busy trying to survive school and not think about the fact that Brody is at the ranch right now.

He's texted me a few times, even sent a picture or two.

I couldn't give them more than a glance.

It'd be like unlocking Pandora's box or something. The past should stay in the past. I don't even know why he's doing this.

I called him, like I said I would, just before I left. Our conversation was stilted, and I couldn't hide my frustration. I wanted to ask him over and over—why? Why are you doing this? You're only setting yourself up for pain and disappointment!

But I didn't want to argue with him, and in the end our conversation fizzled out with half-hearted "See ya laters" and "Have a good time."

Shuffling in my seat, I press my forehead against the window and gaze down at the clouds, kind of in awe of the fact that we're above them. This is so crazy.

It's epic.

I shouldn't be sulking over this. I should be basking in it, appreciating every little moment—the hum of the engines outside the window, the way the world turned miniature as we rose into the air, the small drink I was served and the little bag of pretzels. And the fact that

Carmen is sitting just in front of me. When she moves, I can catch glimpses of her thick hair, and if I breathe in really deeply, I can smell hints of her perfume.

Who knows when this might happen for me again? I seriously need to enjoy it.

You can't do that if you keep shutting Carmen out.

Fix it, man, or this trip is gonna suck.

I'm right.

I know I'm right.

Now I just have to figure out how to fix it.

Lenny chuckles, then unclips his seat belt. I turn to see what he's doing, curious as he stands with a grin and moves to the row in front of us.

"Let me sit next to Hector. He's gotta see this." He waves his iPad in the air, and I hold my breath when Carmen's head appears and she shoots me a nervous grin.

I smile back, trying to put her at ease.

This is my moment.

I need to make things right before we land.

She shuffles into the seat beside me, curling her leg beneath her so she can lean over me to look out the window.

Her sweet smell wraps around my senses, her delicate skin so close I could lean my head forward and brush my lips across her cheek.

But then she moves back, her brown eyes grazing mine before she murmurs, "I'm sorry."

"For what?" I blink in surprise.

Her cheeks flush, her right shoulder hitching. "For getting in your space. For… having to sit next to you."

The vulnerable hurt in her eyes makes me feel like total crap.

"I want you here," I quickly blurt. "How could you even think...?"

Her shoulders slump, her glum expression breaking my heart.

I sigh and resist the urge to take her hand. "I'm sorry if I've been a little... off the last couple weeks. I..."

Her big brown eyes study me, those full lips dipping at the corners before she quietly asks, "Do you still want to come on this trip?"

"Yes. Oh man, you have no idea." I realize I might be saying too much, and with way too much enthusiasm, so I rein it in, forcing myself to take a breath before I keep going.

What do I say?

How much do I say?

"You've seemed kind of quiet and distracted. I've been worried." She studies me again, patiently waiting for anything I can offer her.

I go for a piece of truth that's been weighing me down. It's a starting point, right?

"My... my brother got hurt." I close my eyes, dodging the flash of emotions that one little sentence evokes. "It kind of threw me."

Carmen's face pales, her eyes rounding with what I can only describe as fear. "Oh my gosh. Brody? Is he okay? What happened?"

I hold up my hand to try and stem what looks to be

panic. "He's fine. He's out of the hospital. He, uh, got shot protecting someone."

Her lips part, her wide eyes glassing over.

"Really. He's gonna be fine. Thank God. It takes a lot to bring a guy like him down." I try for a smile, hoping to ease her reaction, which seems kind of extreme.

I guess she realizes how much Brody means to me. I do talk about the guy a lot.

She sniffs, her lips curling at the corners. "You've been worried about him."

"Yeah." I nod, wishing that's all it was. Michael and Deeks skim through my brain, and I close my eyes. "It's hard not to."

"I get it." She rests her hand over mine and my eyes pop open, wonder stealing any sense of composure and no doubt doing stupid things to my face.

She gives me a tentative smile, dipping her chin. "I thought you regretted saying yes to helping me, but you're too nice to let me down so you were coming anyway."

"What?" The idea completely baffles me. Like I'd never not want to go somewhere with her. "I want to be here. Really."

She looks up, and I smile so she knows how much I mean it.

She flashes me her dimples, and that tension that's been lingering between us starts to ease. "Is someone looking after Brody?"

"Yeah, his girlfriend."

"You didn't tell me had a girlfriend."

"I didn't know. I met her at the hospital."

"What's she like?"

"Pretty cool, I think. I'm still getting to know her."

"Good for him."

"I hope so." I nod, thinking of Indy and wondering if Carmen has heard of Castle Shaw. Do I tell her my brother is dating the daughter of a billionaire?

Carmen removes her hand from mine, running it down her braid and grinning at me. "I'm glad someone's there to look after him while you're gone. You'll be back soon enough, and then you can check on him for yourself."

I let out an awkward laugh, then quickly try to catch it before I give myself away.

Check on him?

Not likely.

Brody will be in Montana when I get back. He's there frickin' now. The idea sits like a stone in my stomach.

"Jake? Are you okay?"

"Yeah." I look her in the eye and try to smile.

Focus on Carmen. Just her. Don't waste this trip thinking about the ranch.

"So…" Carmen tips her head, a glint coming into her eyes as she grins at me. "Tell me more about Brody and what happened." She bites her bottom lip, her confidence wavering for a moment. "I mean, if that's okay. Only if you want to talk about it."

Her playful grin has gone into hiding, and I wish it wouldn't. It's like she was trying to get some banter going but then accidentally picked a really serious topic and didn't realize until she'd said the words.

It's kind of adorable, so I lean forward and whisper, "I don't mind telling you."

Her eyes glow with warmth again, and she shuffles in her seat so her body is angled toward me.

"I won't tell anyone. You can trust me."

I know.

I can feel it all the way to my core and wish with every fiber of my being that Carmen was mine. I'd love to win her over, but having Hector right there will make it challenging. I feel a little bad for wishing they'd break up, but from everything I've observed, Hector can't make Carmen's dimples show the way I can.

That's gotta mean something, right?

Oh man, I have to make this trip count.

Which is why I start talking, and I don't spare the details. By the time we fly into Minnesota, Carmen knows everything about Indigo Shaw and how my brother saved her life.

8

A FLUTTERING OF BELIEF

SPENDING the rest of the flight talking to Jake made time disappear. I can't believe everything Brody went through. And Indigo Shaw, for that matter. I felt like I was listening to the plot of a movie, not some actual event that took place only miles from where I live.

It's kind of chilling in some ways.

There are some crazy people in this world.

Evil. Death. I wish they didn't exist.

As I unbuckle and collect my carry-ons, I try not to think about people dying as we shuffle off the plane.

I call my mother as we're walking through to baggage

claim, which eases her first worry—her daughter flying on a plane that could potentially crash.

"I'm glad you're safe, *bebé*. Give Alejandro a kiss from me."

"I will, Mamá."

"And call me when you arrive at the park tomorrow."

I look to the ceiling, clenching my teeth but agreeing anyway. She won't let me get away with less. She has to know her baby girl's safe or she just might lose her mind.

Jake collects my bag for me, and I take it with a smile while Hector and Lenny grab the rest of the gear and load up a baggage cart. I walk beside Hector, slipping my phone away and flashing him a quick smile as he pushes the cart through the double glass doors.

I spot Alejandro immediately, and childhood memories wash over me as I pick up my pace and wrap my arms around him.

"Carmen! *Estás tan hermosa*."

I laugh and take the compliment, patting him on the back and telling him he's beautiful too.

"*Y tú tan grande*." I pat his muscly arms and shoulders. He's huge now.

"It's been ten years since I've seen you. We've both grown up." His expression falters, sadness sweeping over him as he softly murmurs, "I'm sorry I couldn't make the funeral."

I shake my head. "It was so unexpected, and hadn't seen each other in such a long time."

"Still, he was my best friend as a kid. I think I spent more time at your house than my own sometimes."

I laugh, but the sound is watery and uncontrolled. Biting the inside of my cheek, I quickly turn away, introducing my childhood friend to the rest of the crew before I start bawling.

Each member shakes his hand while I pretend my insides aren't roiling. Alejandro and Ademir were only a year apart at school. We used to play together all the time, but then they moved away, and it was reduced to the odd catch-up if they happened to be in San Francisco. I think it happened twice, and before this trip, I hadn't actually spoken to him since my brother died.

It's so good to see him again. But it feels strange without Ademir. If my brother were alive, he probably would've joined this trip just for the fun of it. If he'd been stateside, that is.

If he were here, my parents wouldn't worry so much.

I wouldn't worry.

Glancing at Hector, I think about Papá's words and how he thinks my boyfriend will keep me safe. And I'm sure he will. But not the way Ademir could have. He was my protector, my big brother, my best friend.

My eyes dart to Jake. The beautiful smile stretching across his face as he shakes Alejandro's hand and tries out a little Spanish warms my heart. It pleases my old neighbor too, and they share a laugh, making me realize that Jake has filled a space Ademir left behind. Hector may be my protector now, but Jake's become my friend. A very good friend.

I never really had too many friends growing up. I didn't seem to need them. I was born an introvert, and we spent most weekends hanging out with family. My cousins were my besties, and in spite of the four-year age gap, Ademir and I were close. I had friends at school, girls and guys, but no one I was super close to. I've maintained contact with some of my high school buddies, but I don't know. I kind of adore my study group, and Jake's the main reason why.

Lydia, Cohen, Marty, and Andre are awesome value too, but on the odd session Jake can't be there, I always feel it.

Oh man, I'm so glad we got to talk on the plane, that he said yes to this trip because he actually wants to be here. It was nice hanging out with just him. I mean, Hector and Lenny were in front of us, but for a moment, it felt like Jake and I were the only people in the aircraft.

I liked it. I want to spend more time with just him.

Although I probably shouldn't.

Hector takes my hand as we walk through the skyway that connects the terminal to the parking garage. I glance down at our connection, a cold I can't explain rushing through me.

After loading all our bags into the trunk, I climb into the back seat between Lenny and Jake. Hector took the front seat and is peppering Alejandro with questions.

"It's over six thousand square miles." Alejandro laughs as he answers Hector's questions about the topography. "Plenty to explore. We'll be spending the bulk of our time in the Boundary Waters Canoe Area. We'll paddle for the first part tomorrow and then portage to a spot where we can set up camp. I've got a couple places mapped out that will be perfect for filming."

"Portage?" I ask.

Alejandro nods. "The whole wilderness area is basically lakes and rivers connected by these short trails—portages—through the woods."

"So we bring our canoes with us?" I'm trying to envision what this will look like.

"Yep. We bring everything with us. Trash, you name it. Nothing stays behind."

Jake flashes me an excited smile. I grin, happy that he's as enthusiastic as Hector. Reaching forward, I pat Alejandro's shoulder. "Thank you so much for helping us out this way."

"It's my pleasure. It'll be nice to get back to the BWCA."

"Why'd you stop being a ranger up there?" Jake asks.

"I met a girl." He grins into the rearview mirror, and my heart turns all mushy. Alejandro had mentioned Donita to me on the phone. Initially, she was going to join us, but then a work thing came up and she decided to stay in St. Paul. The way he spoke about her, that sparkle in his eyes right now... they must really be in love.

I gaze at Hector in the front seat, but he doesn't turn to look at me. He's focused on his phone.

"She sounds wonderful," I say. "She must be really special if you moved to be with her."

"She is." He goes quiet for a moment, then smiles at me in the mirror again. "She's totally worth it. I'd do anything for her."

I can tell he means it.

"I am looking forward to going up north, though. And hanging out with you, lil' *vecina*."

Jake looks at me.

"Neighbor," I murmur.

"So, *vecino* would be the masculine?"

"Yes." I bump his arm with my elbow. "Seriously, all this time and I never knew you spoke Spanish."

"I don't speak much."

"You should've told me."

"I didn't want to admit it and then have you think I was really good at it or something. I made that mistake once. Walked into a store overhearing the owner speaking in Spanish, so I thought I'd strut my stuff. I walked up to the counter and said hello, then told him it was a nice day. He grinned and started talking in high-speed Spanish, then looked at me expectantly."

I stifle a giggle, pressing the back of my hand against my mouth.

"It was so embarrassing. I just stood there blinking at him, and he shook his head like I was some hopeless show-off. Then his gorgeous daughter or niece or whoever she was walked up and started laughing at me." Jake shakes his head, his cheeks tinging pink. "I've never tried it again."

I let the laugh free, just a short, happy sound that makes him grin.

"*Amo tus historias. Me encanta que lo intentaras.*" I say it softly so the rest of the car can't hear me.

Jake listens carefully, obviously trying to work out what I said.

"Something about stories, and I missed the second part."

"I love your stories. I love that you tried."

"Tried," he whispers. "*Intentaras.*"

"*Sí.*" I give him an impressed smile.

He grins back. "I need to talk to you more often in Spanish. If anyone can help me improve, it's you."

I love that he said that. I love his blue eyes on mine. They're so bright and hypnotic. I'm caught within his gaze until Hector clears his throat.

I jerk and glance into the front, but he's turning away, asking Alejandro how much longer we're driving for.

"The motel's about twenty miles away. I thought we could split the difference so the drive tomorrow is a little shorter. You guys can just relax for a while."

I lean my head back against the seat and gaze out the window. Dusk has fallen, stealing the light from the sky, and as the outside turns black, my eyes slowly blink closed.

It feels like only moments later when the interior car light comes on. I squint and lift my head, my body flushing with heat when I notice my head has been resting on Jake's shoulder.

"Sorry," I murmur, jerking upright and rubbing my cheek.

"No problem." Jake's smile is relaxed, which helps to ease my embarrassment.

Popping open the door, I slip out of the car and hurry after Alejandro so I can be there to check us in. I'm in charge of the money and have everything allocated down to the last penny.

When we return, the luggage has been unloaded and we're able to direct people to the two rooms we've paid for. Hector takes my hand and leads us to the one on the right. For some reason, I assumed Lenny would be sharing with us, but he trails after the boys. I glance at Hector's face, but he just winks at me.

Nerves skitter through me as he unlocks the door, and I can't help glancing over my shoulder before stepping through. Alejandro gives me a little smile and a wave. I tinkle my fingers back at him and try not to be disappointed when Jake won't catch my eye and wave goodnight.

Why should he, I suppose.

With a thick swallow, I trail Hector into our room and organize my things for bed.

"We've got an early start, so I think we should turn the light out soon."

"Okay." I bob my head, trying to read his expression and figure out if that's code for *I think we should do it in the dark.*

We started sleeping together last year. Like most of my relationship with him, it just kind of evolved, and after a hot-and-heavy spring break where we spent most of our time in bed, we kind of got it out of our systems and have already transitioned into the "every now and then" kind of sex.

It doesn't actually bother me.

And that fact should probably bother me, right?

I'm nineteen and in a long-term relationship with a really handsome guy. Shouldn't I be trying to jump him any chance I can get?

I guess I've known Hector for a really long time. I wonder if that has anything to do with it. He and Ademir were friends from school, and they'd put up with me tagging along whenever they hung out. They were both really sweet about it, never minded the kid sister thing. I was quiet and amenable so I wasn't a bother to them.

Even though Ademir graduated the year before Hector, they still kept in touch. He was at the funeral. One of the first to arrive. And even weeks later, he kept coming over. Kept checking in. The summer after I graduated high school, he started coming over even more. He'd show up unexpectedly to whisk me away. I went along, appreciating the distraction. It didn't hurt so much when we hung out or he took me along to his parties. I didn't have time to wallow when I was busy, and so our relationship just kind of evolved. From big brother's friend to boyfriend. I don't even remember when it became official, but by the time I started at Stanford, I was Hector Cox's girlfriend.

We just became.

And now we still are.

"I know you scored a nap in the car, but I need my sleep." Hector walks out of the bathroom, whipping off his shirt and jeans. I gaze at his firm body and sensible black boxer-briefs. He slides into bed and smiles at me. "Hurry up. I want to turn the lights out."

"Of course."

Slipping into the bathroom, I brush my teeth and get changed into my pajamas. The room is already dark when I step back into it. I slide into bed beside Hector, rolling over and staring at the curtains. His arm comes around me, and he pulls me back against him before kissing my cheek.

"'Night, *señorita*."

I smile at the one Spanish word he never gets wrong. "*Buenas noches.*"

We spoon for just a few minutes, and then he rolls over, a light snore coming out of him only moments later.

Geez, we're like an old married couple already.

Is this really what I want?

I mean, I guess I don't want some guy pawing me when I'm not in the mood. This is better, but...

But what, Carmen? What do you really want?

I stare into the darkness until my eyes have adjusted and I can make out shapes and shadows in the room.

I don't truly know what I want.

I know what I *don't* want, and that's to hurt my parents. To hurt Hector. He's not a bad person. But is he the one?

Does *the one* even exist? Or is that just some pipe dream romance novelists invented?

As my eyes drift closed, the questions continue to swirl through my brain, along with a pair of mesmerizing blue eyes and a fluttering of unexpected belief.

9

SHUTTING UP NOW

Jake

THE FLUTTER OF WINGS, the tuneful call of the birds, and the distant running of an ambling river creates the perfect soundtrack for our portage to our campsite. We've already spent the morning paddling to our exit point, and I was able to capture the beauty on film. My Panasonic Lumix digital camera is really easy to manage and proved, yet again, to be an excellent purchase.

I shared my canoe with Alejandro, and he gave me running commentary on the surrounding area, proving what an awesome ranger he once was. I think he misses it a little, but he's still doing some cool stuff in the Twin Cities with getting urban youth engaged in the outdoors.

It really suits him. The guy is knowledgeable and engaging. It's a double-win.

I can see aspects of Carmen in him when he talks. Even though they're not related, they have this strong Hispanic vibe going, and you could easily mistake them for cousins or something. Maybe that's why I like him so much. Or maybe it's just because he's a super friendly guy. I couldn't imagine people not liking him. He's similar to Brody in that sense. People just kind of gravitate toward their natural charm.

We ended up talking for way too long last night.

It was a nice distraction and a million times better than lying there and obsessing over what Carmen and Hector were up to in their room. I didn't realize they were sleeping together, which is probably kind of stupid considering how long they've been together. Maybe my brain just didn't want to accept it, so I played pretend.

But I couldn't pretend last night, couldn't even face waving goodnight to Carmen; I was too busy wishing I could replace Hector. What I'd give to be the guy slipping into bed beside her.

I shut my eyes and force my brain back to safer territory, like the fact that Alejandro loves rock climbing. I've only ever done indoor climbing, but I'm pretty good at it. Alejandro has already offered to take me to an outdoor rock face next time I come to Minnesota.

"You'll love it, man. Taylors Falls or Tettegouche. Your choice. They're both great climbs, though not for the faint of heart." He grins at me. "I can see you're a climber. You've got the perfect physique for it."

I guess it was his polite way of saying I'm skinny. People always have them—lean, wiry, lanky, slender. I get it, I'm not a giant like Brody, but I can hold my own. Unless it's hand-to-hand combat, and then I kind of suck. I could never throw a decent punch, but I guess that's what I had Brody for.

A smile tugs at my lips, but it quickly fades as I imagine where Brody is right now.

Montana.

The ranch.

How could he do it? Go back to that place?

Are the stones around the hearth still stained with Grandpa's blood?

I don't think I could step foot through that door without seeing it all again. Without reliving that terror, the look on my father's monstrous face as he shoved Grandpa away and accused him of stealing us, the wrath turning his eyes black as he tried to choke Deeks.

"We're nearly there!" Alejandro calls from the front. "We'll set up camp, have a late lunch, and then we can get some filming in."

"Sounds good." Hector puts his thumb in the air, and I force myself to focus on the things around me—the crunch beneath my hiking boots, the smell of pine, the crisp air so fresh and vibrant.

We really are in the heart of the forest, the middle of nowhere. It's like we're the only people on Earth. It gives me an idea of what it must have been like for indigenous people as they hunted and lived off the land, taking care of the gifts nature offered them and looking after each other.

It makes me think of Grandpa again.

But the good times.

The way he taught us everything he knows about the ranch, about how to care for the animals, work with the natural resources we had available. He respected the land, the cattle, the horses. I always loved that about him.

"Carmen, you can get the food ready, right?" Hector says. "The guys can set up the tents."

I frown.

Hector did not just say that!

What is it with guys who think women should always prepare the food?

Hector probably grew up in one of those houses where Mommy lived in the kitchen and looked after everything house related while Dad was in charge of going out to work. Talk about a flashback to the fifties. Haven't we moved on from that?

I roll my eyes when Carmen nods. This is why Hector bugs me. He's old-school, and I hate the way he treats Carmen like his little woman.

I don't see them together that much, but the snippets I've caught always make me think it. He drives her to school most days, like she can't drive herself. He picks her up from study group like she's incapable of walking outside the building without him opening the door for her.

I guess those are kind of gentlemanly gestures, but I don't know.

Maybe it's just me, but I think Carmen's stronger than he

thinks she is. But she's also sweet and accommodating. She isn't one to make a fuss and is happy to go along with everything. I just wish everyone could take a step back and give her the chance to realize she's tougher than she appears.

I see it in her sometimes. That spark. That fire. When she gets all passionate about learning something new, or she's organizing everyone with her timetables and study plans. She's smart, and she can project so freaking well it's like she can see into the future. She's able to envisage, work things out, get the bigger picture.

I wonder if Hector has any idea how brilliant she is.

The people in her life just need to give her a chance.

Like her mom, even. She called *again* when we were leaving the ranger's station. We'd just picked up our permits and gotten the latest—weather updates, animal sightings, anything to be aware of. I read information boards and some of the history of the BWCA while Alejandro logged our plans with the ranger. When he was done, Carmen peppered him with questions, even thinking of something he'd forgotten. He blushed and returned to the desk for more information. It was pretty freaking awesome.

We were just about to get into the canoes when Mrs. Díaz phoned to have one last goodbye before we got out of cell phone range. I could feel Carmen's forced patience, see it in her tight smile as she reassured her mother she'd be safe.

"Yes, Hector will look after me." She glanced at him over her shoulder, and then he took the phone off her and went into some long-winded prattle about how he'd never let anything happen to her.

Okay, so maybe I'm being a little harsh. If I was lucky enough to be Carmen's boyfriend, I would protect her with everything I had, but I'd also treat her with the respect of knowing she'd probably be able to take care of me too.

Where's the belief? The faith?

Carmen's freaking amazing, and I don't think they always see that.

"Here we are." Alejandro comes to a stop in a small clearing. "We'll pitch the tents here, in a circle." He indicates with his hand, then points behind him. "Down that way is a great spot for filming. About thirty minutes uphill and we'll come to a stunning vista. You can have that in the background while you talk."

Hector nods.

"That's perfect." Carmen grins. "We talked about getting a few shots like that. Maybe we could film from two different angles and you could cover a couple of the scenes you wrote."

"Leave the direction to Lenny. He knows what he's doing," Hector quips before crouching down to unpack the tent.

Carmen's cheeks flush, but she doesn't say anything, instead focusing on her pack and pulling out bags of the food we prepared before leaving this morning.

I frown at Hector, who just happens to glance over his shoulder and spot me.

"What?" He frowns back.

I want to give him a piece of my mind and tell him to start treating his woman like the intelligent, helpful person she is, but I don't want to cause a scene.

Carmen's big brown eyes are watching me, and I'm pretty sure she'd be totally humiliated if I call her boyfriend out for being a dick.

So I just shrug and get busy with my tent. "Nothin'. I didn't say anything."

Hector shakes his head like I'm weird before firing a quick look at Carmen.

She turns away from him, getting out a picnic blanket and plastic plates.

While she gets busy creating an outdoor dining experience, the rest of us pitch the tents.

I'm sharing with Alejandro, which is fine by me. It's better than Lenny, who snored like a freaking freight train last night. I guess I'll still hear him through the fabric of the tents, but at least he won't be right beside me.

"Why don't you go give Lenny a hand? His tent isn't supposed to be sagging like that," Alejandro murmurs.

I turn around to see what he's talking about and snicker lightly. Heading over to Lenny, I offer my help.

"Yeah, sure." He nods, then sniffs and steps away like I'm a manservant accompanying him on this trip. I pitch the rest of the tent alone while he sits and talks with Hector.

They're going over the script for the scene we're shooting this afternoon. Alejandro takes a seat beside Carmen, and they chat logistics while munching on beef jerky and premade veggie wraps. As soon as I'm done, I grab the plate Carmen made for me.

"*Gracias, cocinera.*"

She grins while Alejandro lets out a little chuckle. Carmen and I share a wink, which makes me feel a million times better. I sit to check over my camera gear while I eat.

After a minute, I feel eyes on me, so I glance up and spot Hector giving me a stare-down.

Swallowing my mouthful of food, I hold his gaze for a moment, wondering what the hell his problem is. His eyebrows dip together, and he angles his body toward Carmen, holding out his hand for the food.

She pops the plate in his palm. "*Gracias,*" he mutters.

"*Es un placer.*" Carmen smiles, and he leans across and kisses her lips.

I look down, focusing back on my camera like it's the most important thing in the world.

"Gear all good to go?" Lenny takes a seat beside me, leaning in so he can watch me turn it on and check the lens is clean and looking good.

"Yep."

He stays close, hovering around like he's expecting me to screw up at any moment.

It's frickin' annoying, but I hold my tongue.

Carmen doesn't need me getting snarky. I want this trip to be amazing for her, and I won't be the one to ruin it. So I'm gonna keep my mouth shut and be the best cameraman I can be. I'll take Lenny's direction, and I won't complain.

My mission is to make sure Carmen's happy.

As long as Hector keeps his stupid-ass comments under control, that should be a breeze.

"We good to go?" Alejandro brushes the crumbs off his fingers and starts packing up the leftovers.

Carmen helps him while Hector and Lenny get ready for filming. Once the campsite is clear and the food locked away, Alejandro heads toward the narrow trail.

"Don't go off the trail. We've gotten special permission to come here, and we need to respect the forest floor. This trail is hardly ever used, and we want to keep it that way. I know it's narrow, so just watch your step and follow in the footsteps of the person in front of you."

We all nod while I adjust the small pack on my shoulders, then rearrange the camera strap around my neck. Hector charges off after Alejandro with Lenny closely in his wake.

"After you, m'lady." I point to the path with a little bow.

Carmen giggles and curtsies. "Why, thank you, good sir."

We share a laugh.

"Hurry up, you guys!" Hector barks from the front.

I cringe as we both pick up our pace.

"He gets grumpy when he's nervous," Carmen whispers. "This is his first official documentary, and he wants it to be incredible."

"It will be."

"I know." Carmen smiles and nods. "Just forgive him if

he gets a case of the grumpies. He doesn't mean anything by it."

"Good to know." I nod and nearly tell her it's not fair for him to take it out on her, but I don't want things to be awkward, so I walk just behind her and make the decision to step in the line of fire when Hector starts hurling his lightning bolts around.

10

A FUN NIGHT TURNS COLD

Carmen

"AS YOU CAN SEE, even from the glimpse of beauty behind me, our natural world is worth saving, exploring, respecting. We must do everything in our power to ensure this precious land isn't gouged away for profit." Hector stares into the camera with a heartfelt look that matches his outer appeal perfectly.

"And cut." Lenny snaps his fingers with a grin, leaning over Jake's shoulder to check the footage. "Yeah, the lighting is good. Let me see that bit again?"

Jake presses some buttons while Hector catches my eye.

"That was good, right?"

"Yeah. It was great. You look really handsome."

His smile grows. I told him just what he wanted to hear. It's funny, for such a good-looking guy, you'd think he'd have confidence to burn, yet he continually asks for reassurance, fishes for compliments. I'm happy to give them to him. I just find it interesting that he needs them so much.

I step in behind Jake and watch the footage over his shoulder. The lighting is perfect, giving Hector a golden glow that makes him look almost angelic.

"Let me see?" He gently nudges me back so he can step in between Jake and me.

I frown at his back but don't make a fuss, instead checking my clipboard and then my watch.

Alejandro should be back any minute. He's been away for most of filming, scouting out locations for tomorrow. That's the plan. He gets us to a spot, then takes off to find the next one.

We're hoping to film in four different locations tomorrow. It's going to be a really busy day. Glancing at the sky, I notice the red hues of sunset.

"I wonder if we should start heading back. It's going to be too dark to see before we know it."

Just as the words leave my mouth, Alejandro appears.

"My thoughts exactly."

We share a grin.

"Just one more minute." Hector holds up his finger. "Do you think we need to reshoot that?"

"You better be quick," Jake murmurs. "We're losing

the light, and Carmen's got a good point. We don't want to be hiking back to camp in the dark."

Hector mutters something I can't hear.

"What was that?" Jake turns to him with a confused frown.

Hector steps back and turns toward me. "Nothing. Let's just go."

"The shots we got are really great, Hec. I don't think we need to reshoot." Lenny rushes to walk right behind him so they can talk documentary.

I linger back while Jake grabs his gear.

"You okay?" I ask.

"Yeah." He smiles at me.

"What did Hector say to you?"

"I have no idea." He shrugs, looking calm and unfazed. "It was more his tone that surprised me. I think he's annoyed that we couldn't stay and do another take. He loves being in front of the camera, that's for sure. Did you see the way his face lit up every time Lenny said, 'Action'?"

I snicker. "Oh yeah, I did. Hector's always loved having an audience. He used to win speech competitions at school. He was captain of the debate team. I think he got the lead role in a school play once. But yeah, he loves being the center of attention."

"Well, he's good at it." Jake and I share a smile before he indicates for me to take the lead.

I start walking, hoping I haven't said the wrong thing. "He's born to do this job, you know?"

"Yeah, totally. It takes all kinds, right? I'd much rather be on the other side of the camera."

I laugh with him. "Me too. Oh my gosh, definitely."

"Carmen, let's go!" Hector barks from the front.

"I'm coming." I pick up my pace, wondering why Hector's being so grumpy all of a sudden.

As soon as he reaches the campsite, he starts bossing everyone around. I'm put on dinner detail, which Jake offers to help with, but Lenny orders him to go through the footage from this afternoon. The three of them huddle together while Alejandro and I turn a dehydrated Thai curry into an edible meal. I also cut up veggie sticks to go with it.

It's dark by the time we're ready to eat. Alejandro has lit the lanterns and spread them around our camp. I nibble on a carrot stick while Hector uncaps the plastic bottle of vodka he insisted on bringing. I thought it was dumb to have to carry it in and back out again. It's not an essential item, but he argued that a little celebration each evening would make the trip that much more fun. He offers a sip to everyone, but Jake and I aren't old enough to drink, and Alejandro refuses.

"You're not a drinker?"

"Sometimes." He shrugs. "But I can live without it. My Donita used to live with a drunk, and it was scary for her at times. I'd never drink myself stupid, but out of respect for her, we just don't have alcohol in the house. She really hates the stuff."

My heart pulls out of shape listening to Alejandro.

Poor Donita. I wonder if it was a parent or ex-partner. I kind of want to ask but also don't want to pry.

I reach out and squeeze his arm. "You're a kind man."

His smile is soft and humble. "She's an amazing woman. I'd do anything for her. I just love to see her happy."

"Was it a parent?" Jake asks softly, staring at the lantern, a muscle in his jaw working. "That used to drink?"

"No. Her ex-boyfriend. He was a piece of work. I met her while they were still together, and as we became friends, she opened up to me. She was really scared to leave him, but I offered to help her. We moved all her stuff out one weekend when he was away, and we haven't looked back since."

"When was this?" I ask.

"About six months ago. We've been living together ever since. I loved her long before then, and she loved me too. She was just afraid to end it."

I nod, completely understanding. Ending things is kind of terrifying.

Although, it's not like Hector beats me or anything.

I glance across the camping space, watching him tip the bottle back for a decent shot of vodka. He's been kind of grumpy this evening, and I'm not sure why. But he's starting to relax. Lenny says something I can't hear, and it makes Hector laugh.

I turn back to Alejandro, wanting to know more of his story.

"You gave up living here to help her, be with her. Rescue her."

Alejandro shrugs, his smile kind of dreamy. "That's what you do when you're in love. You put the other person's needs before your own."

"But you're still happy?"

"Yeah." He laughs as if he's surprised by my question. "Donita's the best thing that's ever happened to me. We love each other. We make each other happy. Giving up this…" He points around himself. "I didn't hesitate for a second if it meant I could be with her."

The way he's talking, the look on his face… it warms my heart.

We fall into a soft, comfortable silence. I rest my chin on my knees, then glance at Jake. He's staring at me with his beautiful blue eyes. As soon as we make a connection, he jerks and swallows, shifting and turning to dig something out of his bag.

It makes my heart go still.

The way he was looking at me. I've seen it before, I just… It's only now starting to dawn on me. His face. It looked the same way Alejandro's did.

Does Jake like me?

Hope flutters before I can stop it.

No. I can't entertain that idea. It's too good. Too tempting. Too—

"Anyone want to play?" Jake holds up a deck of cards.

"It's too dark to see the cards," Hector mutters, rolling his eyes.

"They're trivia cards." Jake flicks on a little flashlight. "Thought we could do a quiz."

"Ugh. Boring." Lenny goes back to talking to Hector.

Jake sighs and goes to slip the cards away.

"I'll play." I sit up, ignoring the dark look Hector's throwing me. What is his problem?

Alejandro moves a little closer. "Me too."

A spurt of pleasure bursts through my chest. It's an unexpected feeling. Maybe it's just nice to see my old neighbor again, or maybe it's that I love trivia. Hector will never play games like this with me. In fact, he's not really a games person at all, but Ademir and I used to love Trivial Pursuit and competing at Kahoots.

"All right, it's *chicas* versus *chicos*. Let's see who's the biggest smartass." Jake winks at me while Alejandro cracks up laughing.

"Question number one: Hg is the chemical symbol for which element?"

"Mercury," I blurt.

"Correct. One point for Díaz." His smile of admiration makes my chest warm, and I lean a little closer, ready for the next question.

"Which country produces the most coffee in the world?"

"Brazil!" Alejandro and I shout in unison.

"Ooooo. How'm I gonna judge that one? Tie?"

I nod, satisfied with that, then realize we're not actually recording results. "Hang on." I jump up and grab my clipboard, finding a spare sheet of paper at the bottom. "Have to make it official." I smile at Alejandro, who just shakes his head with a grin while I rule up two columns and mark down the score so far.

"In which city was Jim Morrison buried?"

"London? I don't think it was the States," I murmur under my breath.

"Is that your final answer?" Jake's pale eyebrows rise, his look playful and sweet.

I wince. "I don't know."

"Rome." Alejandro offers.

Jake makes a buzzer noise. "Sorry, folks, the answer is Paris. Carmen remains the leading smartass for now."

I giggle while Alejandro rolls his shoulders. "Not for long, *niña*. Donita will never let me forget it if I lose to a college kid. Bring it on, quiz master."

Jake grins. "What was the first state?"

"Delaware," Alejandro answers before I can even open my mouth. "Next."

I give him a mark and hold my breath while Jake asks the next question, and the next, and the next.

After half an hour, the scores are pretty much tied, although I'm two behind. I *have* to get the next three right or I'll never live it down.

Alejandro's general knowledge is amazing, and I'm having so much fun competing with him.

"Who discovered penicillin?"

"Oh! I know this!" I start clicking my fingers. "Um… Alex someone. Uh…"

Alejandro starts calling out names, obviously not knowing the answer but trying to throw me.

"Fleming! Alexander Fleming!"

"Yes, a point for the lady."

I do a little dance on the ground, making a show of adding a point to my column.

"I'm still beating you," Alejandro teases me.

"Not for long." I shake my head. "Next question."

"Who starts first in chess?"

"White!" I yell it out just before Alejandro, but it's close. Jake has to make the final decision, and he points at me.

"Yay." I blow him a little kiss, marking down my score while Alejandro lets out a good-natured groan.

It's all tied up. Only one question to go before I'm beating him.

"I think we should call it a night." Hector stands and walks over to me.

"Just a little longer," I tell him.

"No. We've got an early start. Let's go." He gently nudges my knee with his boot.

"I'll be in soon. Let me just finish the game."

"You guys are being so noisy, no one will be able to sleep if you don't wrap this up." Hector leans over my shoulder and taps my sheet. "You're all tied. Let's just leave it at that."

His breath smells like vodka, and I lean away from it, wrinkling my nose.

"Just one more question, man." Jake pulls out the next card with a flourish, but Hector quickly squashes the fun with a harsh bark.

"I said now! We're going to bed." Taking my arm, he helps me to my feet.

Jake's eyebrows dip into a sharp V, and I can see him getting ready to argue.

"It's all good." I force a smile, not wanting to cause a fight. That's the last thing we need. "Hector's probably right. We have an early start."

I hold out my hand to Alejandro. "Nice playing with you."

"To be continued." He shakes my hand with a grin, but the smile fades as he looks past me to Hector.

"*Está bien. No hagas un escándalo.*"

Don't make a fuss. Just don't make a fuss.

Alejandro and Jake are both looking kind of dark right now.

I tuck the clipboard under my arm and force another smile. "I'm excited about tomorrow. Should be a fun day."

"I'm excited about tonight." Hector pulls me against him and lands a sloppy kiss on my cheek. "Time to get it on in the wilderness, right, angel?"

I push him away, horrified that he just said that in front of everybody.

What the hell is wrong with him right now?

He's never normally like this.

He laughs and brushes his hand down my cheeks. "Lighten up. It was just a joke."

Taking my hand, he pulls me toward our tent, and I can barely see past the heat of humiliation scorching my vision.

We are so not having sex tonight. Even if he wasn't being a first-class jerk, I wouldn't do it. How inappropriate is this setting? The others would be able to hear everything.

"Why did you say that?" I whisper as soon as our tent is zipped shut.

He gives me a withering look and mutters, "It was only a joke."

"It was embarrassing."

"Oh, come on. I was just having a little fun." He leans over and tries to kiss me, but I push him away.

"I am not having sex with you tonight."

"I know that! I said I was joking! What is your problem?"

"You," I whisper before I can stop myself.

He goes still, his glare dark and heated. "What?"

"You shouldn't treat me like that. You intentionally embarrassed me in front of my friends."

"Stop overreacting." He rolls his eyes, kicking off his shoes and sliding into his sleeping bag. "It was a joke!"

"It wasn't funny, and it makes me—" I bite my lips together before I say too much.

This is not the time or place.

"Makes you what?" he snaps.

Or maybe it is.

I stare at him in the lantern light, the lump in my throat like a freaking boulder.

"Not want to be with you anymore," I whisper so softly I wonder if he actually hears me.

He does. The look on his face tells me so.

His scowl only deepens, but now it's got this hurt mingled with it, and I have to look away.

"You're only pissed because I embarrassed you in front of Jake. You hate the idea of him knowing we have sex." I look up, surprised by the venom in his voice. "Because you'd rather be having sex with *him*."

I think my cheeks just caught fire, but I play dumb anyway. "What?"

"You think I'm blind? Stupid? Just your dumbass boyfriend?"

"I... Hector, Jake and I are just friends."

"Whatever, cheat."

My mouth drops open with a gasp. "I've never cheated on you. I wouldn't do some—"

"I'm drunk," he snaps, cutting off any chance of an explanation. "I'm not talking about this right now." Flopping onto his back, he turns away from me, yanking up his sleeping bag to cover his shoulders. "Let's just forget it. This weekend is too important to screw up with your emotional bullshit. We can talk about our relationship when we get home."

The temperature in the tent feels like it just dropped a thousand degrees.

I slip into my sleeping bag, a cold chill running through me.

Hector thinks I've been cheating on him?

I'm insulted. Wounded.

But maybe he's a little bit right too. I may never have acted on my emotions, but I've liked Jake for months. I guess this is the first time Hector's really seen us hang out so much. He obviously doesn't like it.

Crap. I shouldn't have said what I did.

The rest of this trip is going to be so horrible if Hector is grumpy the whole time.

And what about when we return?

A spike of worry blooms in my chest. My parents. They'll be devastated if Hector and I break up. They'd be mortified if they thought I was some kind of cheater.

But it's not like that.

Closing my eyes, I clench my teeth against the nausea rolling through me.

What have I done?

11

SECRET KISSING IN THE WOODS

Jake

I CAN HEAR MUFFLED ARGUING from Carmen's tent, but I can't go over and interrupt. It's not my place. I shouldn't interfere.

"Sucks, right? When you like someone and they're with someone else? The *wrong* someone else."

I still, Alejandro's words washing over me.

Should I pretend I'm just asleep?

I hate talking about my feelings, especially with some guy I barely know. I mean, he's nice and everything, but it's not like he's Grandpa Ray or one of my brothers.

Cooper.

I wonder what he'd have to say.

I always used to go to that guy for advice. I'd hang on his every word, soaking it all in. The amount of times I sensed he was giving me one of those life lessons I'd take with me forever.

"Jake?" Alejandro whispers. "You awake?"

I stay quiet.

"I think you are, and you don't have to talk to me if you don't want to. Just know that I get it. Watching Donita with Jaimon always killed me. I mean, he was a douche. A total asshole. Hector's not like that. Well, not to the same extreme. But I can sense the vibe between you and Carmen. I can tell you like her. Maybe Hector can see it too."

"So what am I supposed to do about it?" I murmur, then wince. I wasn't supposed to engage!

Alejandro's sleeping bag rustles. "If she likes you as much as you like her, she'll figure out that Hector's not the one. You just have to be patient, man."

"What if she never breaks up with him?"

"After the way he acted tonight, I wouldn't worry about it. Carmen's not an idiot."

That's true.

I hold in my sigh, not wanting to give away how heavy this sits on me. I've liked her for so long, occasionally felt that spark between us, but she's always been with Hector. It was never an option.

But what if they did break up?

What if she got together with me?

The thought makes my lips curl at the edges. Through no control of my own, my imagination takes charge, and I picture Carmen in this tent with me. Just me. No one else. She'd lie beside me, her luscious hair draped across my shoulder, her smooth cheek pressed against my chest. I'd run my fingers lightly over her arm, a soft caress. Then she'd look up at me and I'd dive into the depth of her eyes, drawing her close, exploring her mouth, her jaw, her shoulders with my lips.

I've never kissed a girl like that before. Not really.

I've had the odd fumbling kiss—junior prom and then at that party Brody made me go to. They were both kind of disastrous, but it wouldn't be like that with Carmen.

At least I hope it wouldn't.

Getting hot and heavy with her would be all kinds of perfect.

My mind jumps to a different forest—the woods out back, the northern end of Barrett Ranch.

Cooper had taken off at random times over the summer, and I got curious. I followed him, all stealth, and after losing him for a while, I came across my big brother—my hero—making out with some girl.

It was the first time I'd seen anything like it.

Tongues in mouths, hands gliding over the curvy bits, a soft moan that sounded kind of sweet and happy, but ew!

I was horrified. My twelve-year-old brain couldn't wrap my head around it.

Why was Cooper touching that girl's breasts?

Wait! It was Ashlyn, Aunt Nell's niece. What was she doing with her tongue in Cooper's mouth?

And why was she moaning like that?

They were standing so close and getting all out of breath and—

A branch snapped beneath my boot and I jolted, my eyes bulging as Cooper whipped around, his hazel eyes zeroing in on me, like he could see through tree trunks without even trying.

I opened my mouth to try and explain myself, but no sound came out.

Cooper tipped his head to the sky, ran a hand through his hair, and murmured something to Ashlyn. She went a little pink, then pecked his cheek.

"I'll see ya later."

The look she gave him made my nose wrinkle.

As she walked away, Cooper turned to me, his hands on his hips. "Jake, what are you doing?"

"Uh... I..."

"Come out of there."

I stepped out into the open, shoving my hands in my pockets as I watched Ashlyn take off down the path. She was kind of skipping like she was happy about something.

"Why were you spying on me?" Cooper didn't sound mad, but his voice was serious, his gaze kind of stern.

"You kept taking off all the time, and I wanted to know where you were going."

"Now you do. Although, I don't really want anyone to know."

"Why? Are you not supposed to be squeezing her breasts?"

He let out a choked laugh and rubbed the back of his neck. "I wasn't squeezing them, I was just feeling them."

My nose wrinkled again.

"She didn't seem to mind it." The smile on his lips was triumphant as he turned to look at the tree they'd been pressed up against.

"Your tongue was in her mouth." I gagged. "It looked kind of gross."

"It wasn't." Cooper turned back to me with a laugh. "When you're older, you'll understand."

"So girls like that, then? Having their private parts touched and your tongue in their mouth? What else are you supposed to do with them?"

Cooper frowned. "They're not toys you play with, Jake. You don't just go doing that with anyone. You do it with a girl you like and one who wants you to do those things to her."

I thought on that for a minute, mulling it over in my brain. "So, Ashlyn said to you, 'Cooper please touch me and make me moan'?"

Cooper started laughing again and shook his head. "Something like that."

"Huh."

Swinging his arm around my shoulders, he rubbed his knuckles over the top of my head until I told him to quit it.

He eased off but kept his arm around me as we ambled home.

"The main thing you have to remember with girls… women… is that they deserve your respect. You don't yell at them, demand they do stuff, treat them like crap. You have to make them feel like they're special and important, because they are."

He went on, talking about how women are equal to us and we should never make them feel smaller or less capable.

When I look back, I think he was basically describing the opposite of what our father was.

"And you never hit girls," I finished for him.

He clenched his jaw and nodded. "Never ever."

We went quiet for a time, until we breached the tree line and saw the ranch house in the distance.

"So, how do you know when you've found the right girl? The one you're supposed to ask about breasts and tongues?"

Cooper grinned, then covered his mouth as if he was in on some private joke I didn't understand.

"What?"

"Nothin'." He composed himself, then got kind of serious. "Mom always said I should marry someone who could be my best friend too. Someone I could be myself around and not feel judged for it."

"Like Ashlyn?"

He shrugged. "She's pretty cool. We get on great. Talking to her is easy."

"So you love her, then?"

He laughed and winked at me. "It's just a summer romance. I'm too young to be in love."

"But she's your friend, right?"

Cooper gave a thoughtful pout, then nodded. "I feel like I could tell her anything."

I started to smile. "Maybe you do love her, then."

"I sure love kissing her." His smile was so big it made me laugh. It seemed like the right thing to do. "Just promise me you'll never tell anyone about me and Ashlyn, all right?"

"I promise." I held out my pinky finger, and he wrapped his around mine.

It was a vow I wouldn't break.

"Why don't you want to tell?"

He shrugged. "Don't know. Guess I just want to protect it."

That sounded like a good idea to me, so we wrapped up the conversation before we reached the barn, and as far as I was aware, Cooper's secret stayed safe with me.

I wonder what Ashlyn's up to now.

Did she cry when she found out Cooper had disappeared?

Or maybe he went to find her?

Who knows? My gut wrenches every time I let myself think about Coop leaving us like that. He didn't even say goodbye. And it was right off the back of Grandpa dying too.

I'm not sure I'll ever get over it.

I wonder if Ashlyn did.

How could he do it to her?

She used to come visit every summer. Probably to see him. And then he just left.

I wouldn't do it.

Not to Brody, and definitely not to Carmen.

If I could ever win her heart, I'd protect it with everything I had. Oh man, I'd love to rescue her from this relationship she's currently trapped in. I mean, I guess she's not trapped, but… I don't know.

I just can't help thinking she'd be better off with me.

Is that arrogant?

Maybe she really does love Hector.

I probably shouldn't interfere, but that look of humiliation on her face tonight… That was just mean. Hector should not have said that to her, even if he was joking.

It definitely wasn't respecting her, and it pissed me off.

Hopefully that muffled argument means they won't be having sex tonight. I hate the idea of being this close to them when they're doing something like that.

Not when I'd give anything to be that guy instead.

I wouldn't take it for granted, that's for sure. Being with Carmen would be the most amazing thing. I know it would. I'd give my all to make sure she was happy and…

My mind drifts again—Carmen beneath me with a loved-up smile, her—

A soft snap makes my eyes ping open. I tense, homing in on the sounds around me.

Was that crack a branch or stick?

Is someone out there?

I hold my breath, listening for noises until all that surrounds me is nighttime nature.

Must have just been an animal.

Man, I'm glad Alejandro's with us. I know a lot about nature, but most of it's from reading and watching Bear Grylls. I haven't done much hiking, and none in isolated areas like this. Alejandro was a ranger. He's experienced this stuff, and I have nothing to worry about.

My eyes drift shut, images of Cooper, Hector, Carmen, and Ashlyn swirling like a vortex in my mind. My dreams are disrupted by dark trees and animal calls. Then a gunshot explodes in the back of my mind. Then blood. So much blood.

12

_____

JEALOUSY IS AN UGLY BEAST

Carmen

I DIDN'T SLEEP VERY WELL and woke up feeling like crap. It sets things up for the morning. Obviously last night's display and the argument to follow have not been forgotten.

Hector won't even look at me when I hand him his breakfast. The entire camp is pretty subdued, so I keep my eyes trained on my clipboard to make sure we're organized for the day.

Alejandro is forcing lighthearted conversation. Jake engages a little, but it peters out pretty fast. Eating is nearly impossible, so I give up on my eggs and focus on my coffee instead.

As we're packing up to go, I notice Jake grab a bunch of extra snacks—trail mix and granola bars. When he sees me watching, he just smiles and murmurs, "In case we get hungry later." His bag closes with a quick zip, and he pulls it onto his back.

"Right, guys. This way to the next spot." Alejandro leads the way, and we trail along quietly.

Jake isn't saying much, and when I glance back to check on him, I spot the gray bags under his eyes and his pale complexion. He mustn't have slept well either. I wonder why.

Nerves dance in my belly. I press my hand against it, trying to calm myself.

Just focus on the things you need to do to get through this day. Don't project ahead.

I bite my lips together and start with just my footsteps, one after the other. Just one task. One thing at a time. It helps keep the anxiety at bay. That's what I was told.

Be present.

Don't worry.

Keep control.

That's what I have to do today. If I think too hard about last night or why everyone is so sullen this morning, it'll just send me into a tailspin of questions.

Am I really breaking up with Hector?

What will my parents say?

How is Hector really going to take it?

And what about Jake?

Does he like me?

What if I just imagined that, and then I'll be all alone? No Hector. No nothing.

Which is worse?

Agh! Cállate, Carmen!

I take my own advice and shut my thoughts down. Those questions will be the death of me. Seriously.

We reach a patch of sunlight, a small clearing drenched in warmth and practically glowing.

"This lighting is amazing!" Lenny gapes.

"I know, right? Such a great location." Alejandro points to the trees beyond. "If you stay here long enough, you'll spot some deer for sure. Maybe even a moose if we get lucky."

I strain on my toes to see past Lenny and try to spot some.

"I'll leave you guys here and go on ahead, scout out the next location."

I give him a thumbs-up. "Sounds good. Thanks."

We share a brief smile, and the rest of the day is taken up with filming. It actually goes pretty well. Alejandro moves us to four different locations, each as beautiful as the one before it.

We return to camp for a late lunch, then hit the final spot of the day.

Tensions seem to ease as we work, and it doesn't rear its head again until we stop for lunch. I don't know where to sit. I'm not sure if Hector wants me beside him, but I don't think he'll appreciate me by Jake either.

So I kind of sit in the middle, separated from the two of them as if it doesn't bother me. Lenny tries to strike up conversation, but Jake's not in the mood to chat, and Hector's in snippy mode. Lenny gives up and mutters something under his breath, while I home in on my beef jerky and try not to gag on the dried meat sticking to my throat.

This is awful!

Alejandro wanders back, and I hand him some food. He sits with me, looking confused by the layout of everyone, but is wise enough not to say anything. So, like breakfast, lunch is a total downer. I practically jump to my feet when Lenny suggests we get on with it.

Yes! Working is good. Let's work!

And we do. The next hour or so isn't too bad as we film and focus on this documentary.

I'm kind of dreading the final "cut" for the day. This evening is going to suck. I'm looking forward to bed tonight. I'll probably have to share with Hector again, but at least I can face away from him and hopefully be so tired after a full day of shooting that I can fall into a coma.

That'll be nice.

"So, as you can see, it's worth it." Hector gives a cheesy smile to the camera and lifts his thumb.

I can't help a cringe. I've never liked this part of the script. It's like an advertisement or something. We're not selling cars.

"Was that good?" Hector looks to Lenny, who is watching over Jake's shoulder.

He gives a thumbs-up. "Excellent. Yeah, I really liked it."

I wrinkle my nose, not realizing that Hector's watching me.

"What?" He frowns.

"Oh." I blink and wonder what to say. Maybe if I word the truth nicely… "Um, I just think it's… Well, it's a little cheesy. And in that last part, your movements were a little too rehearsed. It didn't look natural. Maybe if you relaxed your shoulders or—"

"It has to be rehearsed or I might say the wrong thing."

"I know. It just sounded like you'd memorized it too much. I don't know if that makes sense."

"Not really." Hector shakes his head, crossing his arms and not even attempting to understand me.

"I just think—"

"I didn't invite you here to think, Carmen. Let the big boys come up with the ideas, all right?"

My lips part, the sting of his words like a slap to the face.

I know he's pissed at me right now, but he's taking it too far.

This is ridiculous!

"I agree with her," Jake pipes up, looking at the camera while he's talking. "You are kind of robotic here. Maybe we could—"

"Of course you would. You agree with everything she frickin' says."

Jake pauses, eyeing Hector carefully before softly saying, "Maybe because she has good things to say."

Hector clenches his jaw, his nostrils flaring.

I appreciate Jake standing up for me, but I don't want to ignite this. He doesn't know what Hector said to me last night. I need to cool this down, and fast.

"Look, whatever. Hector, Lenny, if you're happy with the take, keep it. It's your documentary." I check my clipboard. "Now, do you want to film the next part here, or are we going back to the site we were at before lunch? I heard you mention something about that." I check my watch. "We should probably get moving before we lose this light. Want you to look good, right?" I can't resist the sarcastic quip, and Hector picks up on it immediately.

Crossing his arms, he gives me a withering glare.

I want to stand up to it, but instead I feel my cheeks get hot and end up looking down at my hiking boots.

"You know there's nothing stopping me from sending your sweet ass home." Hector glares at me. "We can do this without you, you know?"

And the slaps just keep on coming.

My throat burns with anger, indignation... maybe a little hurt.

I swallow and try to sound stoic when I look up to face him.

"Why'd you want me to come, then?" I flick my arms out, my clipboard slapping against my leg when they fall again.

My sweet ass?

He's never said something so horrible to me before.

What a prick!

"Someone has to keep his bed warm." Lenny cracks up

like he's just said the funniest thing. Hector snickers and gives me a hard smile.

That's it!

My eyes start to burn as well, and before anyone can see me cry, I spin and stalk away. I have no idea where I'm going, and I don't freaking care.

It is so over between Hector and me. I can't believe how he's treating me.

I've never seen this side of him before. No wonder I've been having my doubts. Jealousy is so freaking ugly on him.

He told me to wait until we got back from this trip before discussing our relationship, but you know what? Screw that! I am *not* sharing a tent with him tonight. I don't care how awkward it gets. I'd rather sleep outside with the bugs anyway.

I duck into a clump of trees, jumping off the path and not even caring. I just want to get away from him right now. I need to think!

Dumping him is going to make the rest of this trip so awkward.

I don't care!

Yes you do.

If Hector's insufferable now, he'll be heinous if you dump him in front of everyone, especially in front of Jake.

I close my eyes, tears threatening to spill over.

Hector's worked so hard to make this documentary dream come true. Can I really ruin it for him?

But he's being a jerk!

He is, and I'm totally justified.

Aw, crap. He's being a jerk because he thinks I've been cheating on him.

I haven't.

I haven't done anything wrong.

Sure, I like Jake... a lot, but I would never act on my feelings.

A tear slips free, and I let it trail down my cheek.

I don't know what to do.

Hector and I are over. Or we will be over. I guess I just have to pick my timing, and maybe in the middle of his first film shoot isn't it.

I'll just have to tell him to get over himself, and if he can't do that, well, then... I'll have no choice.

Sleeping with the bugs it will be.

13

HECTOR THE DOUCHE

Jake

"THAT WAS A DICK MOVE, MAN!" I grip my camera, my knuckles turning white as I aim a heated glare at Hector. "Why do you talk to her like that? She's your girlfriend. You should treat her better."

His scowl matches mine, his upper lip curling with disgust. "You should know all about that."

"What's that supposed to mean?"

He scoffs. "I'm not blind. I've watched you two on this trip. You want her, and maybe she wants you too. Flirting right in front of my face! How long's she been cheating on me?"

Unbelievable.

I shake my head, struggling to form words.

He really thinks that little of Carmen? That she'd do something like that to him?

The guy is freaking clueless!

Wait.

I still as a thought finally filters through my irritation and hits home.

What did he just say?

She wants me?

My indignant surprise is being tempered by that beautiful idea. Hope sands down the edges, cooling my anger and lowering my voice.

"She hasn't cheated on you," I assure him. "If you knew her at all, you'd know she'd never do something like that." And the anger's back again. A quick spark that's a blue flame in my chest. "She's a good person, and you treat her like shit. I can't believe you'd think so little of her when she's put up with your crap for so long."

"My crap?" He glares at me like the oblivious idiot he is.

"You treat her like your little woman. Like she's supposed to worship the ground you walk on. Do you have any idea how intelligent she is? How resourceful? She's capable of so much more than you ever give her credit for, but all you can ever think about is you and how she can best serve you!"

His eyebrows dip into a sharp V, but I don't miss the hurt flashing across his face.

"You just don't see her." I shake my head. "And she's

too nice to call you on it." My jaw works to the side as I try to smooth out my emotions again.

I see her.

I'd never have to make her call me on anything, or if I did, I'd give her the space to do it. Make her feel like she could be one hundred percent honest without bruising my sensitive ego.

Hector's a dick!

"You don't deserve her, man." I shake my head.

Hector's nostrils flare, his fists clenching into two tight balls.

I've seen it before.

Faced it down.

Like Steve Rogers before he became Captain America, I can take a hit.

Although, Brody (my Bucky) isn't just around the corner, ready to step in and save my ass.

"Okay, this isn't achieving anything, and we're losing light. It'll be dusk in a couple hours. Let's just get the next take and we can sort this domestic out later." Lenny's diplomacy sucks.

Like I'm going to film anything without Carmen.

With a deep scowl, I walk past Lenny, flicking his hand away when he tries to grab my shirtsleeve.

"We're not doing this without her," I snap over my shoulder, stomping through the forest in the direction she went.

I can't see her anywhere nearby, so I pick up my pace, hoping she hasn't veered off the trail.

Carmen's smart enough not to get lost. She's probably

hiding away so she can cry in private. As much as I want to give her that space, I also need to check that she's okay. I need her to know someone is on her side.

I can give her a hug or just stand there and listen... or if she doesn't want to talk, I'll just be beside her. Whatever she needs, that's what I'll do.

And when she's ready, we'll return to Hector the Douche and figure it out from there.

14

SEEING THE TRUTH

Carmen

I SLASH the tears off my cheeks, bashing branches out of the way as I head deeper into the woods. I know this is a stupid, senseless move, but I need to hide for a minute.

The trail's to my left. I'm keeping track of it in the back of my mind. I'm not lost.

I just want to be alone.

With a little sniff, I wipe another tear away with the back of my hand. I don't want to cry. It always gives me a headache and makes my eyes red and puffy.

Besides, I'm smart enough to know I have to return soon, and I don't want to be a blotchy mess—the poor, pathetic woman who can't keep her emotions in check.

Grrr!

The sound of someone crashing through the brush behind me makes me pick up my pace.

I don't want to deal with Hector right now.

He'll no doubt want to smooth everything over, and I appreciate the sentiment, but... I can't right now. I want to stay mad with him. I don't want him to be sweet or thoughtful like he can sometimes be. It'll be easier to end it that way.

End it.

Crap! Why does this have to be so hard?

I don't want to hurt anybody, and Hector's jerk behavior is probably just that. He's jealous and hurting... and I'm the cause of that.

But if I don't end it, will this just linger and get worse?

He obviously sees how much I like Jake, or can sense our connection. Things are never going to be the same again, and if he somehow insists I can't be friends with Jake anymore, then...

A cold despair sweeps through me.

"Carmen!"

Jake.

I turn at the sound of his voice, against my better judgment slowing to a stop.

A moment later, I see him ducking beneath a tree branch and spotting me. His smile is relieved and sad and sympathetic. Everything I need it to be. My nose starts to tingle with a fresh batch of tears.

"You okay?" He says it so softly, so sweetly. His hand gently glides down my arm, his blue eyes studying my face like he can feel whatever I'm feeling. "Sorry Hector was being such a dick."

I shake my head with a little sniff. "He's never been so rude to me before. I know he can be hard work sometimes, but he's above and beyond on this trip. I don't know what his problem is."

Jake purses his lips, running a hand through his floppy hair. It falls straight back over his forehead as he adjusts the strap of his camera.

"What?" I whisper, heat rising up my cheeks as I wonder what Hector said to Jake after I left.

"Well, I think, maybe…" His eyes dart to mine before flicking away again. "He doesn't like that we get on so well. He thinks you're cheating on him."

My shoulders deflate with a heavy sigh. "He said that to you?"

"Yeah, but I told him you'd never do something like that. I told him a few things, actually." Jake winces, and my heart bursts with something warm and gooey.

He stood up for me?

My lips toy with a grin I can't stop. "Like…"

His laughter is breathy and kind of embarrassed, the pink hue on his cheeks only making my heart glow brighter. "Like he was a dick for treating you that way, and if he wants to keep you, he should stop acting like a clue-less moron. He should look, and… and really see you." His eyes rise to mine, and he drinks me in like I'm something special. "See how incredible you are and… and treat you the way you deserve to be treated."

His voice has dropped to a breathy whisper. There's a

pulse in my throat—fast and yearning, like my heart wants to run right out my chest and wrap around Jake's.

It's hard to find words with these heady feelings running through my body, and if I don't break this connection we've got going, I might accidentally lurch into his arms and kiss him.

Dipping my chin, I run the toe of my hiking boot over the dirt and murmur, "I bet that went down well."

Jake hisses. "Lenny jumped in, and I took off before I got smacked in the face."

A little giggle spurts out of me. I slap my hand over the sound. I should not be laughing over this. Hector and I are breaking up. It's not funny. It's sad and will no doubt come with bucketloads of drama, but...

But Jake thinks I'm incredible.

He stood up for me.

With a thick swallow, I lower my hand and get caught in Jake's gaze again.

He's letting me see—the affection, the admiration.

How long's it been there?

How long's he been hiding it for?

I shouldn't be with Hector. I want to be with you.

I'm this close to opening my mouth and letting out the big confession when an ugly sound makes me flinch.

I can't quite place it, but a chill runs down my spine as I look right and strain my senses for more.

There it is again.

A slapping of... flesh?

A punch. A groan of pain maybe.

"What is that?" Jake whispers, stepping up to my side and lightly resting his fingers on my elbow.

"I don't know."

"Do you think we should"—he gives me a dubious frown—"check it out?"

"We better." I'm nodding before I even realize I am, but instinct is telling me someone's in trouble. I didn't even know anyone else was out here in this deserted place.

Nerves rocket through me as Jake's hand glides down my forearm, then wraps around my fingers. With a little squeeze, we step forward together, creeping up slowly as another pitiful groan pulls us forward.

15

A PACK OF WILD DOGS

THAT GROAN IS UNNERVING the hell out of me, but I'm glad Carmen wanted to check it out.

How do you walk away from a sound like that? It'd niggle me for the rest of the day, night... months, even.

We can't just take off.

Carmen's long fingers curl around my hand, her grip tightening as we carefully move forward, wanting to investigate before deciding what to do. I step over a stick, wary of making any sounds.

Another crunching of knuckles on flesh.

No groan this time.

Is that a good or bad thing?

Holding my breath, I pull Carmen a little to the left, finding a pocket of trees and brush we can hide behind. Squinting through the leafy branches, I can make out a group of men.

They're in a small clearing just ahead of us. We're about one hundred yards off the trail, and the secluded spot would probably be an idyllic patch of sunlight to rest in, but the golden hue this afternoon is highlighting a brutal ugliness that makes my chest spasm.

Five hunters with rifles aimed at a bloodied man on his knees.

The big leader-looking guy is standing over the poor man, his hand clenching his shirt collar, his fat fist poised for another punch. There's blood on his knuckles, but I can tell it's not his. The wet, red gleam belongs to—

"Alejandro," Carmen gasps, her eyes bulging as she gapes at her friend.

I flinch and take another look, shock rocketing through me. What the hell is going on?

"You thought you could just have her? Huh? Is that what you thought?" The guy punches Alejandro, and I wince as the ranger's head flops back, a fresh spurt of blood firing out of his nose.

He doesn't make a sound. He's beyond groaning. Not even a whimper. He just sways on his knees, looking ready to pass out.

Clenching my fist, I try to figure out what to do. I need to stop this, step up and get these guys away, but if I walk out there, I'll come directly into the line of fire. And so will Carmen.

I'll get pummeled, and who knows what they'll do to her?

Instead, I quietly lift my camera, inching away from the trees so I can get a better shot, and start recording. At least Alejandro can use this as evidence when he wants to press charges. These guys will no doubt be done soon. They'll hike away, leaving Alejandro to fend for himself. That's what bullies do.

They'll think they've left him for the bears, but Carmen and I can step in and get him back to the ranger's station.

This documentary trip is over or on pause for the foreseeable future. Hector will just have to lump it.

"JT, please," Alejandro lisps, blood coating his bottom lip when he tries to speak. "I didn't steal anything. She wanted to be with me."

The man growls while his buddies curl their lips and practically snarl at Alejandro. A pack of wild dogs. I scan my camera around their faces, making sure to get shots of each of them. I can't get all the faces clearly, but the police might be able to work with partial profiles, and I'm getting their clothing too. That should help.

The trees are still obscuring my view a little, so I inch to the left in order to capture the guy on the end. His bushy mustache is straight out of the '80s. It'd be laughable if this whole situation weren't so freaking scary.

The big guy—JT?—whips a hunting knife from the back of his belt.

Carmen tenses beside me, pulling in a short breath. I catch a glimpse of her out of the corner of my eye and notice the way her chest is rising and falling—too fast, too erratic.

Steadying the camera in one hand, I brush her arm with the back of my fingers.

Just breathe, Carmen. It's gonna be okay.

"If she's not with me, she's not with anyone," JT barks.

I grip the camera again, hoping the sound is carrying enough to capture all of this. My fingers are slick as I take one more quiet step and get a better angle on Alejandro's attacker.

He's a brute of a guy—wide, square face covered in dark whiskers. His look of wrath could be captured on a comic book villain. He's definitely got that vibe going on. Intimidation. Power. He's putting Alejandro in his place. Making sure he knows the rules.

Alejandro sways, his cheek twitching in obvious pain. His right eye is swelling shut, and there's a gash on his cheekbone. He's a mess. I won't be surprised if something is broken.

But we can fix that.

Bones heal.

I'm anxious for this JT guy to say his piece and piss off. I wish there was a way I could hurry it along. Poor Alejandro needs medical attention. Maybe if we cause some kind of distraction, alert them to the fact that someone might be watching, they'll freak out and take off.

Or they'll aim those rifles toward you and start firing.

I wince, not willing to take that chance.

"You don't—" Alejandro rallies, spitting out his words

with obvious effort. "You don't touch her. You'll never hurt her again."

JT pulls him close, leaning down and spitting in his face. "That's not your call to make."

"I won't let you near her!" Alejandro's shout is feeble and weak, and blood drips off the end of his chin, falling like rain onto the placid grass. He grabs JT's forearm, trying to fist his shirt, but the big guy just flicks him off with a growl.

Alejandro starts to fall, but JT grabs him, wrenching him close with a look that turns my bones to ice.

"You won't have a choice." His harsh whisper is followed by an act of pure rage. So swift, so surprising, I nearly drop the camera.

The hunting knife plunges into Alejandro's neck. The poor man's eyes bulge in disbelief while the air around us seems to evaporate.

No one can fathom this.

The other hunters, they're stunned. They're just standing there with their jaws dropping to the ground while JT rips the blade back out and steps away.

Alejandro flops forward, hitting the grass with a dull thud.

I stare at the screen, barely able to form a coherent thought.

All I can see is the blood dripping off that blade.

16

_____

HE'S DEAD

Carmen

"NO!" I whimper, the sound punching out of me as I stare at Alejandro.

He's dead.

That man killed him!

I gape at my friend's limp body. I can't see his face, but I'm sure he's dead... or about to be. This weird choking sound comes out of him, his shoulders convulsing, then shuddering still.

Everything's suddenly quiet.

There's nothing.

Nothing but an ache so strong and sudden that I buckle over, gripping my knees and biting my lips against the shout I want to unleash. A cry of horrified grief roars through me, making me shake and tremble.

This can't be happening.

He's dead.

Just like Ademir.

They're both dead. Dead!

"Alejandro. Alejandro!" I don't realize I'm sobbing his name until I glance up and notice five heads turning in our direction.

"What was that?" one of them barks. The man with the bald head and wide green eyes. "Did you hear something?

"Someone's there." The mustache pulls his gun around to the front of his body and peers into the forest.

Do we freeze? Hope they don't see us?

"Shit! I see something! I think it's a camera! Someone's filming this!" He starts running toward us.

Jake lowers the camera, his eyes bugging out when he glances down at me.

I'm still kind of frozen in my little spot, trying to pretend this is all just a nightmare I'll wake up from.

"Get him!" The shout makes me flinch.

Jake snatches my wrist and starts yanking me back the way we came. Veering right, he pulls me toward the trail. We'll be more exposed, but we can make quicker ground on the wider, smoother surface.

"Run," he urges me between breaths. "Fast. Let's go. Come on. Come on."

I pick up my pace, letting go of his hand and pumping my arms as we make a beeline for the campsite.

We need to get Hector and Lenny. Get the hell out of here.

Without our guide.

Holy crap! Holy crap!

Alejandro's dead.

17

ALL THAT MATTERS

Jake

CARMEN'S KEEPING pace behind me, but we need to go
faster.

I can hear—feel—the hunters gaining on us, and after
what I saw a few minutes ago, they will have no qualms
about finishing their business.

That guy killed him in cold blood.

Did he mean to do it?

I don't know. His rage was pretty potent; maybe it was
a blind act of emotion, but I doubt he's going to start
thinking straight now.

He'll be on the warpath, especially if he knows how
much I captured.

Holding my camera steady, I try to run and form a plan at the same time.

Get Carmen to safety.

Get this footage to the authorities.

Try to remember where the hell we are so they can recover the body.

Three simple tasks, right?

Just three little things.

My chest is burning as I grab Carmen's hand again and pull her a little faster.

The camera keeps bouncing against my chest, hurting me, but I can't ditch it until I get the SD card. All the information is stored on there, and it'll be a million times easier to transport.

My camera.

It kind of kills me that I'm going to have to dump it, but what choice do we have?

It's like escaping a burning building. You don't have the luxury of gathering your precious possessions. It's your life, so you run because that's all that ultimately matters.

"That way! Check the trail!" The voices are faint, which means we've made some distance, but as soon as they hit the trail, they'll speed up.

Carmen veers us left, and we head into the woods again, cutting the angle to get back to the campsite.

Hector and Lenny will hopefully be there, or will have heard this commotion and come to find us. We can't just leave them to the mercy of these psychopaths. We need to stick together, help each other to get back to the ranger's station in one piece.

We can ditch everything at the campsite, come back for it later.

All that matters now is the SD card and getting out of here alive.

18

BE SILENT. BE STILL.

Carmen

WE BUST into the campsite where Hector is sulking on a rock and Lenny is pacing.

The second he spots us, he flicks his arms in the air.

"Finally! Nice of you to frickin' show up!" He's pissed, and maybe he has a right to be, but there's no time for this now.

"Alejandro's dead!" I blurt, my voice quaking. "They just killed him!"

Hector jerks to his feet, his face draining of color. "What?"

The terror I kept at bay in order to run suddenly thunders through my body, and I start retching. My stomach convulses in painful spasms as I pitch forward and heave. I don't hurl chunks, just ugly-sounding coughs and saliva. I've hardly eaten a thing today, and nothing but bile and panic wants to come out of me. I spit on the ground, tears flooding my vision as I alternate between dry pukes and quaking sobs.

Someone's holding my side, supporting me, keeping me upright.

"We have to get the hell out of here. Now!"

Jake.

His arm's secure around my waist, his voice barely quavering as he takes charge.

"Those guys aren't far behind us."

"What guys?" Lenny's totally confused. "What the hell is happening?"

"Just go!" Jake shouts just before the noise of running feet comes thundering forward. "Shit!"

Wrenching my arm, Jake pulls me behind his tent, hurtling over a thick, fallen tree trunk and crouching us into hiding. We press our bodies into the earth, ducking low so our heads can't be seen. It helps that the ground slants away, giving us a little pocket to hide in.

"He's serious! Run!" Hector shouts.

I can't see him bolting away, but I'm a little surprised he's not coming to join us. Instead, he must be running the opposite direction, Lenny in his wake by the sound of the scampering feet.

"Should we go after them?"

"No, it's too late," Jake whispers. "They're too close. We just have to stay put and stay silent."

I press my hand into my stomach, praying I don't start heaving again. My body is quaking, and I can't seem to control it.

"Breathe. Deep breaths." Jake curls his fingers gently around my arm.

I look at him, focusing on his calm blue gaze while I force air through my nose.

His eyes smile at me, and it helps me to keep going, keep breathing—one inhale, one exhale.

I can do this.

A rush of noise approaches on our left, and I squeeze my eyes shut.

One inhale! One exhale!

Don't freak out!

Crunching boots make me tense.

Harsh puffing.

Angry voices.

"Where'd they go?"

"Get that camera! This whole thing will turn to shit if someone's seen our faces."

"Where'd they go?"

"I don't know!"

"Well, go look for them! Don't just stand around like some idiot!"

Feet thump in different directions. I'm not sure how many go where, but I press my body even further into the ground. Straining to place noises, I hold my breath and try not to make a sound as I press my face against the damp earth. It's a chilly ice pack against my skin, matching the frosty blood that seems to be running through my veins right now. My fingers are shaking, my belly still quivering as I close my eyes and see Alejandro's blood-soaked face again.

"You two, search the camp."

Oh shit!

Jake rests his hand lightly on my back, then quietly shifts his position. Working slowly, with stealth-like movements, he lifts the camera strap over his head.

The sounds of wrenching zippers and gear being kicked aside makes me flinch.

I focus my eyes back on Jake. His fingers are trembling as he tries to pop open a flap on the bottom of his camera. It springs up and he pulls out the SD card, shoving it into his pocket and placing the camera in the dirt.

"What are we looking for, JT?"

Another crash as something metal is thrown away. The kettle? The cooker?

"Anything that'll be useful! Maybe some ID or something we can use!"

Bile surges up my throat—a scorching-hot sick that makes my stomach spasm again.

ID? What are they going to do if they find us?

I hold in my whimper, cover my mouth, and start to pray.

Oh Dios, ayúdanos, por favor. Mantennos a salvo. No nos dejes morir. Por favor, deja que Alejandro sea llevado al cielo.

I beg God to keep us safe and not let us die. I ask that Alejandro be taken to heaven. The Spanish words flow easily through my brain as I cry out for aid.

Haznos invisibles.

I ask for invisibility, squeezing my eyes shut and silently whispering the request over and over.

They shouldn't come around this way. Jake's tent was pitched right against the log; hopefully they'll assume there's no space to hide back here.

"This isn't the way it was supposed to go!"

"Shut up!"

"I thought we were just scaring him, warning him to stay away from Donita, but you had to put a knife through his neck!"

"I said shut up! He deserved it!"

"What if they find the body?"

"They won't. We'll hide it, and no one will know."

"Someone will come looking for him, and if someone he knew filmed it, there's no way this won't catch up with us."

"Stop panicking! We find that camera, get rid of the evidence, and we'll be fine. As for his missing ass, they'll assume an animal attacked him or something. Just calm the fuck down and go hide the body! Go!"

With a string of muttering curses I can't really make out, feet thump away from the campsite, leaving one… or maybe two people behind. How many chased after Hector and Lenny?

Oh my gosh, are they okay?

A gunshot rings out in the distance. I grip my mouth, pinching so hard it hurts. But I can't make a sound.

Was that Hector?

Did they shoot him?

Jake's muscles coil, but he doesn't make a sound. His

blue gaze reaches mine, and I cling to it. He holds me steady, his face so calm as he touches his finger to his lips. I nod, promising not to make a sound.

A radio clicks. "Did you get 'em?"

"Maybe? Going to take a closer look."

I close my eyes, setting a few tears free. They trail down my cheeks, and I dare not move to brush them away. I can't budge, make a sound, give anything away.

"Dammit. Sorry, man. It was a deer. No sign of them."

"Well, keep looking for 'em. We need that camera. You do whatever it takes to get that footage."

There's an ominous pause before the radio clicks again. "Whatever it takes? Are you saying... *whatever*?"

"Anything you have to. I'm not going to jail over that asshole. He got what was coming to 'im."

My stomach starts to shake and writhe—my terror is being overridden by a healthy rage.

How dare he!

Alejandro was a good man!

My friend.

Dead.

My insides churn, making the rest of my body shake. Soft fingers brush my cheek, and I open my eyes.

Jake's pools of blue draw me in, his lips curling just a little at the edges.

If I could read his mind, I'm sure he'd be saying, "Stay with me. We're gonna make it. You just have to stay with me."

I nod, taking in a soft, quivering breath and nodding even harder.

Jake sits up a little, moving like a cat as he slowly pivots to the balls of his feet. He beckons me with his hand, and I follow suit and move to a crouch.

Another crash rings out as something is flung out of one of the tents. We use the noise to mask our own, creeping away from the campsite and into the dense forest beyond.

We stay low, as out of sight as possible until we're well away from the site and the trail.

As soon as the noise feels far enough away, we break into a sprint, careening through the forest. My legs burn as we run up short hills and stumble and slip down boulders and into dips. We need to find something that will give us some direction—a stream, another trail, something to guide us back to the ranger's station.

And we need to not get caught.

Fear sends a shard of ice right through me, and I pick up my pace, ignoring the stitch in my side and my tight chest, forcing my aching legs to keep going.

Run, Carmen. Just run.

19

ONLY THE BEGINNING

WE RUN for I don't know how long, pushing our bodies to the limit.

I hurtle over a log, and Carmen's right beside me, scrambling around a crop of trees. My backpack slaps branches, my forearms take hits as we blindly charge through the woods and unchartered territory.

Adrenaline is pumping so strong I'm almost light-headed, but I can't stop.

Not yet.

We need more distance.

Space.

A safe moment to think this through.

I have to keep Carmen safe. That's paramount.

Second to that is getting this footage to the authorities. The SD card in my pocket feels like a rare jewel, a precious diamond that must be protected at all costs.

I can't believe they killed Alejandro.

I've only seen death two other times. I thought watching Mom waste away to cancer was the worst thing in the world, but then came that stormy night where Grandpa was shoved into unforgiving stone and Dad was shot by Cooper.

This seems worse.

The knife through the throat was so brutal, blatant, cruel. There's something more personal about death that way. I can't even explain it, but it shocked me to the core.

And I can't let them get anywhere near Carmen.

I wasn't able to save Grandpa, but I will save this woman. I don't care what it takes.

And then we'll get justice for Alejandro. He deserves it.

Shit, he was such a nice guy.

Why?

Why does life have to be so damn unfair?

That asshole—JT—must be the ex-boyfriend Alejandro mentioned. I can't remember what name he said, but I'm sure it started with a J.

It must have been the man he rescued Donita from. The drunken asshole.

And now he's dead for it.

Shit.

Jumping around another tree, I leap over a log after

Carmen, then let out a shocked gasp, my feet hitting air, then slamming into the steep slope.

Carmen yelps and starts tumbling, her body rolling over while I slip and slide, bumping into a tree root before slamming into a flat patch of concrete. Well, not concrete, but it feels like it.

I lay there for a second, letting the dull ache travel through my body before finding the willpower to move.

With a soft hiss, I roll over and wonder if anything's broken.

"Carmen," I whisper, worry coursing through me as I turn my head to check on her.

She's on her back, blinking up at the canopy of trees.

"Are you okay?"

"Yeah," she rasps.

"Nothing broken?"

"I don't think so." She goes to sit up, then winces and stays put. "Just bruises."

Pretty big ones, I imagine. My body's feeling pummeled right now.

I go still and listen out for the sounds of running feet, but I can't hear anything.

Hopefully those wild dogs have gone the other direction. All we have to do now is find our way out of here. The chances of crossing them have got to be slim, right?

The chances of finding your way out are probably slim too.

I squeeze my eyes shut, not wanting to entertain that negative thought. But it's there now. It's starting to turn over in my mind. The prospect of being stuck out here.

The thought that no one will ever find us in this vast wilderness.

My nerves rattle like broken glass. I can't go down that rabbit hole.

Pulling in a breath, I force myself to work on what I can control, on the sounds of the forest around me. For now, we're safe. The only sound we're hearing are the birds and the rustling trees.

It helps me take another deep breath. Gives me the strength to commando-crawl to Carmen's side.

"You sure you're okay?" I brush a lock of hair off her cheek, pulling a dried leaf out of it. "You're definitely not hurt?"

She shakes her head. "I'm all right."

But then her chin bunches, her lips trembling as she lets out a shaky breath and starts to cry.

Oh crap.

What do I do?

Um… I'm not quite sure how to play this. I'm not exactly schooled in the ways of women and what to do when they start crying, but…

Sitting up, I gently take her wrists and help her off her back. Then I go to wrap my arm around her shoulders.

"Don't," she whimpers. "If you hug me right now, I'm gonna fall apart. I'm gonna cry and snot all over you."

I drink her in for a moment, loving that beautiful face more than I ever have before.

"C'mere," I whisper, giving her arm a soft tug and pulling her onto my lap.

She flops against me, a soft whine coming out of her before she grips my shirt and starts bawling.

Cradling her head against my shoulder, I hold her steady, trying to keep all the pieces together while she shakes and shudders, weeping out the shock, the pain. She needs to do this. It's all part of it. You have to let that train of disbelief and horror ride right through you so you can process and find the strength to keep going.

Resting my cheek against her head, I let the tears burn my eyes too. My throat swells as I squeeze my lids shut and try to come to terms with what we've lost.

It's not over yet, either.

This isn't the end.

The sick dread in the pit of my stomach is warning me that there's a lot more to come. The fight for our lives is only just beginning.

20

PROMISES MADE AND BROKEN

Carmen

I CRY until I'm completely drained and my head is pounding.

With a little sniff, I wipe my nose with my shirtsleeve —gross—and try to mop up my face.

Jake is still holding me. I don't actually mind that he ignored my request not to hug me. I needed it. I was just worried about ugly crying all over him. But he didn't seem to care about the tears and the snot, the heaving of my stomach. He held me like I mattered. He's still holding me.

Pulling in a quivering breath, I find my voice again. "We've lost them, right?"

"Yeah. We're safe for now."

I nod, my throat closing up again.

For now.

There's something so ominous about those words.

"I'm terrified," I softly admit.

Jake squeezes me a little tighter. "Me too."

For some reason, knowing that makes me feel better.

Sitting back, I study his face and wonder yet again how he can give me a calm smile. It's just touching his eyes, but it's still there.

"You don't look terrified."

"Looks can be deceiving." His smile grows a little bigger, flashing me white teeth before going away. He clenches his jaw and gazes around us. "It's good to cry, to process, but we can't let fear own us on this one. We have to push forward. We have to keep it together."

My head starts bobbing, but then it can't stop. Swiping my damp cheeks with the back of my hand, I try to get myself together, but my head won't stop going up and down. Great. Now it's getting faster. And my hands are shaking. And it's getting hard to breathe again.

"Hey." Jake gently stills my face, his thumb resting on the tip of my chin.

I squeeze my eyes shut, battling a fresh wave of horror as images of that knife plunging into Alejandro's neck massacre me.

"Carmen, look at me."

I force my eyes open, confronted by his blue gaze—so soft and caring. I cling to it like a life preserver.

"We're going to get out of this. I promise. I would

never let anything bad happen to you. We're gonna make it."

"You don't know that." My eyebrows wrinkle. "You can't promise me something like that."

Life is too uncertain.

I don't want him making rash statements that just aren't true.

Broken promises hurt. They're lies that wound and puncture. They're hope killers.

We have no guarantees out here. We're lost in the wilderness with no way of contacting anybody. We could starve, get attacked by an animal, injure ourselves. Or those men could find us!

A chill jerks my spine, and I twitch in Jake's arms.

He pulls me against him again, lightly squeezing the back of my neck. With a soft sigh, he tells me, "You're right. I can't promise you... anything." He sighs again, this one heavy with frustration. I go still, my head resting on his shoulder, until he pulls back so he can look me in the eyes. "Except I can." Rubbing his thumb across my cheekbone, he gives me a look of pure sincerity. "I can promise that I'll try. That I'll do everything in my power to keep you safe. I won't stop. I won't give up."

My lips part as my heart one hundred percent believes him.

"Do you trust me?" he whispers.

I nod, surprised by how much I do. If I can have faith in anyone, it's Jake. He's so like Ademir, like...

"Alejandro," I whisper, fresh tears stinging my eyes.

"I know." Jake's rasping voice is his first indicator of real emotion. He's shaken. I can see it now.

I sniff and try to keep the tears at bay.

"But we've got them." Jake gently shifts me off his knee and digs into his pocket, pulling out the small plastic card. "This is going to get him justice."

Justice. It's a poor consolation.

Justice won't bring Alejandro home, just like it didn't bring my brother home.

Justice is worthless.

"Donita." My lips tremble. "She's lost him. He made it sound like they were so in love, and she's lost him."

"I know." Jake looks pained as he slips the card into a zipped pocket of his cargo pants.

"She's lost him." I cover my mouth, imagining what she'll go through when she finds out.

Will she cry the way I did when we got the news of Ademir? Curl into a ball on her bed and never want to unfurl?

Or will she drop to her knees and wail like Mamá? Maybe she'll try to be stoic the way Papá did but fall apart weeks later, sobbing over her eggs and forgetting how to tie a tie or work the blender.

Jake kneels in front of me, cupping the back of my head and resting his forehead against mine.

"I know this sucks. And I wish I could make it go away. I wish this wasn't happening, but we can't change the facts. All we can do is take one logical step after another and find a way out of this. We just have to survive."

I sniff. It sounds impossible.

"We're gonna make it," he repeats, like he's trying to tell himself this truth as well. "We have to make it. Not just for us but for Donita. If we don't bring these guys down, they'll go after her, and we can't let that happen."

I jolt, my head snapping up as his words sink in.

Oh my gosh, he's right.

My eyes bulge as the realization runs right through me, sparking an urgent energy I didn't even know I possessed. It's enough to get me off my butt and help me to stand.

Jake's right.

I can't let Alejandro down. Donita meant everything to him. We can't just leave her to that evil asshole. We have to do something!

Justice—this time around, it does mean something.

We have to save Donita.

We *have* to make it.

Pulling my filthy clothes straight, I look over at Jake and nod. "Let's get moving."

21

BE LOGICAL... UNEMOTIONAL

EXCELLENT. Carmen's coming back.

The murky panic hindering her vision before has cleared. The crying jag did her good, and now she's ready to move on.

Hitching my pack, I do a full circle, taking in our surroundings and wondering what to do next.

I need to get my bearings, and I wish like hell that I'd paid better attention at the ranger's station.

Alejandro took charge, and I was happy to let him, but now it's just me and Carmen.

"Do you have any idea where the ranger's station is? North, south, east?"

Carmen shakes her head. "Alejandro took all the maps and logged our route."

I slip the pack off my shoulders and start digging out my compass. It won't do much good to us if we don't know where we're supposed to be going, but at least it will tell me which way north is.

I watch the needle twitch and finally settle. It's pointing at Carmen, and I nod, then look up and around us.

Trees on all sides. Endless trunks and branches that give me no direction.

"Water. We need to get to water. A stream or river will lead us somewhere," Carmen suggests. "We canoed in, right? So the river will lead back to the ranger's station."

"Yeah, but which river?"

"I don't remember. Was it called Moose River? Or did Alejandro say we might *see* moose by the river?" She gives me a hopeless, defeated shrug, and I feel bad for dumping on her idea.

"You're right, though. We need to find water." Resting my hand on the tree nearest to me, I quickly map out a climb and jump for the lowest branch.

"What are you doing?"

"I'll see if I can get a view from the top." I start climbing.

"Careful."

Carmen's sweet reminder makes me grin, but I do pay attention, carefully selecting where I place my hands and feet.

It's a relatively easy climb, and I'm breaching the top a

few minutes later. The view is breathtaking, and if I wasn't lost and in mortal danger, I'd be in awe.

A vast green table of trees stretches for miles around me. Splashes of water capture the light, probably small lakes with narrow interconnecting waterways, but no clear route or river I can see. I mean, there will be one, since we're in the BWCA, but I just can't see a path from here. All I've got is rolling forest… and dying light.

The sun is heading for the horizon, and I quickly calculate that we've probably got an hour or so before we're shrouded in darkness, maybe even less with the forest cloaking the sky.

I scramble back down and land with a thud by my bag.

"Anything?"

"Forest for miles and a few spots of water, probably small lakes, but no river." I hitch the pack onto my shoulders. "Let's think about this. Superior National Park and the BWCA borders Canada, which is north. We came in at Ely, and we haven't hiked or canoed too far from the ranger's station, so logically, we need to head south."

"Southeast or southwest?"

"That's the part I don't know."

Carmen worries her lip, gazing back down at the compass I handed her. "I feel like south is going to take us straight back to…"

"The bad guys." It's lame, but I can't think of a better word for them right now. "I guess we'll just have to trust the size of this forest. We'll stay alert, keep an ear out for any foreign noises."

"Okay." Carmen's whisper is so soft I nearly miss it.

Taking a tentative step forward, she holds the compass in front of her and starts leading us south, which feels like the way we came.

Struggling back up the embankment, we claw the dirt and strain our muscles until finally we're gripping that fallen tree trunk and hauling ourselves over it.

The light has faded even more in that short time, and we're now making our way through looming shadows. The birds have gone silent, their songs replaced by chirping crickets and the hum of other insects, and the spooky sound of a calling loon. The only way I can identify it is because Alejandro pointed it out the first night of our trip.

Pulling out my flashlight, I spread the beam across the darkening forest floor, but it's pretty feeble. Plus it might draw attention to us. Anything flickering or moving will catch the eye of a hunter and who knows how long they'll stay out looking for us? They're desperate men, and that's the most dangerous kind.

What we need is a decent shelter where we can hunker down for the night. Somewhere obscure and hard to find.

I start scanning for good spots.

"We need to find shelter, and we need to work fast." I let Carmen in on my thinking.

She nods and we pick up our pace, changing our purpose as darkness starts to settle in.

Shit, we better find something soon.

Panic sizzles, teasing the edges of my jittery stomach.

But I can't let it take hold.

I have to cut it off. Be robotic. Unemotional.

Just like I was the night Grandpa died. When we had to stand in that hospital, looking the sheriff in the eye and lying to save Cooper, to save us all. Panic was trying to take me out on all sides, but I couldn't let it.

"What happened to your grandfather?" The sheriff rested his hands on his hips, looking tired, water dripping off the peak of his cap.

Michael swallowed beside me, the sound loud and laced with guilt or pain or despair.

All three emotions were raging in me; I could only assume he felt the same.

"He tripped and hit his head on the fireplace," Michael answered.

"Anyone else at the house with you?"

"Yes, our brothers. They're coming."

The man's forehead flickered with confusion.

"We took off ahead of them to get Grandpa here as fast as possible," I told him.

It was a weak lie, and I was waiting for the man to ask more, but the sheriff just pulled out a notepad from his back pocket, like he was only just remembering that he should probably write some of this down.

"Is there someone I can call to come take care of you?"

"Aunt Nell. Our neighbor," I respond. My voice sounded distant and far away.

"Do you know her number?"

I rattled it off. Grandpa had made us memorize it in case of an emergency.

Like the one we were facing that night.

My stomach trembled, and I had to clench my jaw to keep it all in.

The sheriff walked off to find us some hot chocolate and call Nell just as a doctor came into the waiting area, looking sober. His wrinkled mouth was drawn downward, and I knew. Before he even started talking, I knew.

"I'm so sorry, boys," he murmured, "but your grandfather didn't make it."

I went numb. This cold chill swept right through me, taking all the feeling with it. Michael shuddered, then let out this gargled kind of sob. He slumped into a chair and buried his head in his hands. I just stood there, staring at the wall and blinking slowly.

My brain didn't want to compute in spite of the fact that my insides were screaming.

A loud "NO!" reverberated through my body, a soul cry that eventually buckled my legs.

My butt hit the chair and I gripped the handles, keeping my eyes on that wall and willing myself not to lose it.

Robotic.

Unemotional.

That was the only way.

Carmen's puffing breaths bring me back to the present. I glimpse her face in the dimming light and wonder if I can do it again. How am I supposed to be unemotional with her around? She stirs things inside me that no one ever has before.

Just stay calm. Find shelter. That's all you gotta do.

22

CHILDHOOD GAMES IN THE DARKNESS

Carmen

DARKNESS IS NEARLY over us when I finally spot a cave.

Well, kind of. It doesn't have a back end. It's just some big rocks and boulders that have slipped to form a kind of triangular shelter.

"Is that good?" I point.

Jake's white teeth flash. "Perfect."

Squeezing my shoulder, he then rushes across to the space, quickly checking the integrity of the structure.

"Absolutely perfect." He drops the sticks he's been collecting as we hunted for a good spot. "Come on, let's get this shelter set up, and then we can start a fire. It'll keep us safe from insects and predators."

Predators?

A shiver runs through me. "But what about the smoke... the light? Won't that be too much of a beacon?"

He pauses, and I can't see his expression, but by the rustling of his jacket, I can tell his shoulders have slumped.

"Survival 101," he murmurs. "Shelter, water, fire, food."

"I just don't know if the fire will alert them to where we are." I wince, not wanting to contradict him. He obviously knows what he's doing. I, on the other hand, know zero about this stuff.

A soft tap and snap makes me flinch, and I spin around, searching the darkness for clues. Is it a predator? A hunter?

Which is more dangerous?

What should we be protecting ourselves from?

"You're right." Jake's soft voice spins me back around. "I should have thought about that. Let's, uh... let's at least get the shelter set up. Start hunting around for some big bushy branches we can use to block off the back part of this shelter. It'll stop the wind howling through, keep us warmer, and then we've only got one side to defend, you know?" His voice picks up at the end, like he's trying to be bright and hopeful, but it doesn't work.

The word *defend* rattles between my ears. Sick dread pools in my stomach, but I nod and get to work, hunting the nearby area. My eyes adjust to the darkness, but it's still a little off-putting walking around without clear vision. It doesn't help that my limbs are trembling. Every foreign sound makes me jerk and sends my heart racing.

Thankfully, it doesn't take us long before we're hauling back a few dead branches that are still covered with pine needles. We stuff them up against the back of the shelter, creating a third wall. Jake moves stones around to secure things and then sets up the confined space so we've got room to sit and stretch our legs out.

"How do you know all this stuff? The survival 101 thing?"

"Bear Grylls is my superhero." I can only just make out his grin in the darkness.

"That's right. I knew that. You've watched everything he's ever produced."

"Hey, it's compelling TV."

I giggle, enjoying the slightly lighter moment.

Bobbing down beside him, I stretch my legs out and try to get comfortable. My fingers are shaking as I zip my sweater up to my chin and arrange the back so it's tight against my neck.

"You cold?"

"I'm all right." I force a smile, happy for him to think the uncontrolled shakes are to do with how cold it's getting and not the fear that's clawing up my throat and using my heart as a punching bag. I've never slept a night in the complete wilderness like this. I've never been in a life-or-death situation before. It's hard to stay cool, calm, and logical when reality is pressing in from all sides, terror overriding any sensible thoughts you might be lucky enough to conjure.

I rub my hands together and have to admit that maybe these shakes aren't just from fear. It's going to be a cold night. Without the sunlight and constant running, I'm starting to cool down rapidly. It makes me wish I had more than just my sweater and the light jacket I'm wearing.

"Here." Jake hands me his water bottle. I only sip a little, knowing we have a limited supply. "Hopefully, tomorrow we can find a stream or something. I put some of those purifying tablets in my backpack, so we'll be able to drink any water we find." He takes the bottle back and holds out a granola bar.

"The whole thing?" I ask.

"Yeah, I've still got a few more in here. I packed extra because you hardly ate any breakfast."

I flush with embarrassment that he even noticed.

This morning feels like eons ago.

That safe little campsite, Hector sulking over his coffee, Alejandro wandering off to scout filming locations.

I close my eyes, struggling to finish the bar Jake gave me. But I need to. We have to fuel ourselves for whatever tomorrow will bring.

Scrunching the wrapper in my hand, I tuck it into my jacket pocket, then hunch over, rubbing my arms to try and get warm.

"Here." Jake unzips his jacket and opens his arms wide. "Body heat's the best way. We need to help each other out."

I give him a tentative smile. My mind jumps to Hector

for a moment, his jealous glare, and then the panic on his face just before he started to run.

Away.

Away from me.

I wonder if he made it.

Not wanting to contemplate any other option, I shove the thought aside and crawl across to Jake. He spreads his legs to make room for me, and I tuck myself against him, resting my head on his shoulder and helping him pull the jacket around us both.

It's tight and kind of squishy... but I instantly feel the effects of it. So much warmer.

So this is what Jake's arms feel like.

I guess he's held me a couple times today. Too bad the circumstances have all been so harrowing.

Jake sniffs and adjusts his head. His chin is resting right by my ear, his fingers clasped together across my torso.

A tingle of heat passes through me, this strange butterfly sensation that seems so inappropriate for a time like this. Jake's lips are right there. If I turned my head, I could kiss him.

But I shouldn't want to do that right now.

We're fighting for our lives!

There's a chance we won't even make it through the night.

My chest constricts, my airways starting to close off as that heavy feeling smothers me.

No, I can't think like this. I can't let the ugly in or I'm going to lose it again.

"When I was a kid, my brother and I used to play this game," I blurt.

What?

Where did that come from?

"Oh yeah? What was it?" Jake's voice is soft and smooth.

I stare into the darkness and take myself back in time.

"It was a question game to distract us whenever life wasn't playing fair. If we felt scared, or sad, or sick, or bored even." A smile curls the edges of my mouth. Young Ademir becomes a fresh image in my mind. His messy mop of dark brown hair, his round cheeks with a deep dimple on each side. The game was his idea, his brown eyes dancing as he wiggled his eyebrows at me.

"If you could be doing anything else right now, what would it be?"

"Ademir, I don't want to play." I sniffed and hugged my teddy bear close, tucking it under my chin.

"Come on." He nudged my shoulder. "It'll make you feel better."

"All I feel like doing is throwing up again."

"I know." His smile was glum and sympathetic. "But you said you can't sleep, and this will distract you from your yucky tummy."

I sighed and rested my head on the pillow. "What was the question again?"

"If you could be doing anything else right now, what would it be?"

My feverish brain was struggling to think clearly, but I eventually croaked, "Swimming in a nice, warm ocean with the sun on my face and pelicans diving in the water for fish."

"Nice imagery, sis." Ademir's smile always made me feel like I was the best.

I managed a weak grin, then asked him the same question.

"Me?" He pointed at his chest, then made a big show of thinking it through. "I'd be in Egypt, standing in front of those ancient pyramids watching camels walk by and listening to all the foreign noises around me."

"That sounds fun. I want to do that too."

"Okay, come with me."

"Then where should we go?"

"After that…" He looked to the ceiling, his lips turning into a huge smile. "Let's go to those temple ruins in Cambodia!"

"Carmen?" Jake's soft voice pulls me back to the present. "How do you play the game?"

Ademir's childlike face disintegrates in my mind. I blink and take in my surroundings—a faint owl's call in the distance, a rustling in the forest that could be anything from a bear to a rabbit, the ominous darkness beyond our hiding spot. The small cave opening suddenly feels huge, like a window highlighting us to predators— wild animals and hunters with guns.

I snap my eyes shut and force the words out of me.

"You say, 'If you could be doing anything else right now, what would it be?'"

"Okay." Jake nods, the short whiskers on his chin brushing against my cheek. "And I'm guessing the sillier the better, right?"

I giggle. "It sometimes ends up being that way, but start with the truth." I lift my head so I can look at him.

I can't really see him in the darkness, but I've memorized his features anyway. I know the lines of his face—so refined, like he's been carved from marble.

It makes me feel better, focusing on that gorgeous image.

"Where would I rather be..." He looks up, his Adam's apple bobbing when he swallows—I can hear it. "Maybe a movie theater with a huge tub of popcorn and a Coke-flavored Icee. Watching... some National Geographic documentary, you know, with those sweeping shots of a mountain range or an ocean."

"That sounds fun." I grin, nestling a little farther back against him.

"How about you?"

"I'd rather be lounging in a hot tub that overlooks the ocean with a white sandy beach just two steps away. The salty breeze would kiss my face as I sat there drinking up the sunshine and sipping on an ice-cold pineapple juice."

"Pineapple juice. Nice. That's a great image."

I can't help an impish grin as I wonder what he's picturing. I'm too scared to ask, so I keep my eyes on the darkness and conjure up another scenario.

As expected, things turn silly after a while, and we're

soon soaring to Mars in a high-tech rocket with a monkey in the seat beside us and Earth out our window.

To be honest, that would freak me out, floating around in a vast solar system, but it's better than the peak of Everest, which is what Jake was saying before.

My favorite of his was the horseback riding over fields dotted with cattle, and then my addition of a warm log cabin with a cozy fire and a view of the mountains.

He didn't respond to my suggestion, so I let it slide. In fact, things turned quiet for a while after that, and I thought he'd drifted off to sleep. But when I looked to check, I could tell he was still awake. His silence seemed sad and lonely for some reason, and it made my heart stir.

"Are you okay?" I whispered.

He snapped out of it immediately, swallowing and forcing out a soft chuckle. "Yeah, of course. Let's go to space. Mars. With a monkey."

I laughed and let the silliness take over.

We needed a little silly. A small reprieve from the weight bearing down on us.

I miss my brother.

I wish he was here.

But I've got Jake. And that's really good too.

Turning my head into his chest, I warm the side of my face and let my eyes drift closed. My limbs grow heavy, and I welcome it. Sleep. Sleep will restore me, and maybe if I'm lucky enough, we'll wake in the morning and find this has all just been a crazy dream.

23

SWEET DREAMS TO BLACK REALITY

IT'S A DREAM, I can sense it, but I don't want to let it go because it feels so close to a memory.

Maybe it is a memory.

A good one.

Something from my past that isn't harrowing.

No, it's nice. It's...

"That's my boy!" Grandpa hooted, banging the table with his fist and laughing as I put another plastic wedge into the Trivial Pursuit wheel. "This is why I love being on your team." He mussed up my hair and grinned around the table.

Cooper winked at me while Michael's eyes darted to the last cookie on the plate. The winning team was going to halve it, and by the way things were going, it was gonna be Grandpa and me.

Deeks groaned, slapping the question card down on the table and scowling at Brody.

"What?" Brody nudged him with his elbow.

"He's thirteen!" Deeks pointed at me. "He's not supposed to know what the currency of Poland is!"

Brody laughed. "I've never even heard the word Z... Zl..."

"Złoty," I said for him.

"No one has! Unless you're Polish!" Deeks scowled at me, pointing his index finger at my nose. "You're not Polish!"

I grinned and shrugged. "I read it in a book just a couple weeks ago."

"Well, stop reading so damn much! You're killing us here!" Deeks slapped his hand on the table.

"Oi." Grandpa pointed at him, a silent warning to check his language before he had to drop and do twenty.

Deeks rolled his eyes and snatched the dice, giving them a dramatic shake before dropping them on the table. One bounced onto the floor and I ducked under the table, reading the number it landed on so it'd be fair. You didn't get to roll twice, even if it did fall off the table.

"Green. What's green?" Deeks moved the wheel while Cooper pulled out a question card.

"It's Science and Nature."

Michael perked up, because that was his favorite category. "Can I ask it?"

Cooper passed the card over while Deeks clenched his jaw and nodded.

"If you planted the seeds of Quercus robur, what would you grow?"

My forehead wrinkled. I didn't know that one, but from the grin on Grandpa's face, I could probably have worked it out.

I was guessing tree or something like that.

"Flower?" Brody answered before consulting with Deeks.

"Nope." Michael dropped the card and snatched up the dice with glee. "A tree."

"What?" Deeks slapped Brody on the arm. "You're supposed to check with me first."

Brody shoved his brother away with a good-natured laugh. "Were you gonna say tree?"

Deeks opened his mouth to protest, then chuckled and shook his head. "No. I was gonna say flower."

We all started laughing and ribbing Deeks, who managed to turn bright red before bringing us back to the game.

Within fifteen minutes, Grandpa and I were celebrating our victory.

I felt like a million bucks as he wrapped his arm around me, slapping my back and telling me once again how smart I was.

"The brains of a champion. I'm telling ya. You're gonna go far, son. Real far."

The smile in his eyes told me how proud he was, and I believed him. In that moment, I believed any dream could come true.

Cooper slid the cookie plate across the table. "To the champions go the prize."

He smiled, and I ceremoniously lifted the cookie, breaking it in half and checking the portions were fair before handing the slightly bigger piece to Grandpa. He winked at me before making a big deal of how delicious the cookie was.

Everyone groaned and rolled their eyes, except Michael, because he'd made them.

Grandpa always had a way of making us feel important, turning the ordinary into brilliant and amazing.

"Come on, boys, you clap for the winners now. Do the right thing."

After a sigh from Deeks, everyone broke into applause. Grandpa made me stand and take a bow, and then we all pitched in to clean up and get the house tidy before bed.

"Don't want to be coming downstairs to a mess in the morning."

Grandpa always said that.

His voice still rings inside me sometimes. I can hear it so clearly.

"Wake up, son. Time to open your eyes." My forehead

wrinkles and I sniff, the dream evaporating as realization dawns cool and clear.

I'll never hear his voice again. Not in the real world.

I shiver, trying to shift into a more comfortable position, but I can't. Something's on me.

Someone.

My eyes snap open, and I glance around the shelter, memories from the day before flooding me like some sick, action movie.

It was real.

It was all real.

There's no happy Trivial Pursuit in this place, just murder and a cold sick fear clinging to the edges of every thought.

Well, not *every* thought.

I gaze down at Carmen, still sleeping against me, her luscious hair splayed across my shoulder. My discomfort is a thousand percent worth this moment. Carmen's in my arms again. She was all night. We kept each other warm. We stared into the darkness, talking, playing her "If you could be anywhere else" game.

In spite of all the terror, we found this beautiful moment within it.

Because Carmen and beautiful moments come easily. They're a perfect match.

I brush my fingers lightly down her hair, my jacket rustling softly. The noise might wake her, but I can't help leaning forward to press my lips against the top of her head. She smells of pine and dirt, a little sweat mingled into the mix. She'd probably be mortified if I told her that.

She usually smells of vanilla or jasmine… or something sweet and fruity. Whatever perfume or shampoo she uses, I freaking love it.

But I don't mind the pine and sweat either.

It's Carmen. What's not to love?

Dawn is approaching. Our cave is slowly becoming lighter at the edges—a soft brightening of shapes around me. As soon as Carmen wakes, we need to get moving again.

As much as I don't want to, we have to push forward and find a way out of this place.

But maybe just a couple more minutes won't make a difference. Maybe just a few more moments of her weight on my chest, her soft even breaths filling the space around me, the smooth curve of her cheek capturing me the way it always does.

She's so incredibly beautiful.

She's—

I stop breathing, my body instantly tensing when I hear something approaching. It's a soft, shuffling sound. A movement.

I can't see it yet, but I can sense the danger. Adrenaline surges through me, alerting my reflexes and switching my senses into overdrive.

Something's not right.

Quickly scanning for my pack, I glance to the cave opening and wonder what I could use as a weapon.

I don't even know what I'm fighting, but—

A snuffling snort stills me.

Animal.

Ironically, better than human right now. At least whatever is sniffing around our shelter isn't out to kill us. As long as we do the right thing.

Is it better to be still and hope it goes away?

Wrapping my arm slowly, carefully, around Carmen, I watch the opening.

Stay calm.

Be cool.

You can handle this.

I keep telling myself that until I see a big brown snout push its way into the entrance of our little cave.

Yeah, that's a black bear. I've seen pictures. I know what they look like.

Although... pictures don't really tell you how freaking huge they are!

24

ECHOING GUNFIRE AND SPIKY NEEDLES

Carmen

I'M jolted awake by a quick intake of breath. Or maybe it's the pounding in the chest beneath my ear. Whatever it is, my eyes pop open and I'm instantly alert.

"Stay calm," Jake whispers. "It's gonna be okay."

Those are not the words you want to wake up to, but I do my best to stay in neutral while trying to figure out what I shouldn't be freaking out about.

That's when I hear the snuffling. And the scratching.

And I know.

I smell it before I see it, and I whip my head around to take a look.

"Stay calm," Jake reminds me, clenching my body to

him as the bear's massive claws scrape the ground by my feet.

I yelp and jerk my legs up to my body. The sharp movement makes the bear's head pop up.

It looks directly at us, and I don't know how I'm not peeing my pants right now. Its black, beady eyes stare me down before it steps back and stands tall, letting out a gruff noise that sounds freakishly like a growl.

"Get up, get up, get up." Jake practically pushes me off him.

I roll to the side, nearly eating dirt before I'm hauled to my feet.

"Start waving your hands in the air." Jake lifts his arms and shouts, "Argh!" Stamping his foot on the ground, he shouts again.

"What are you doing?" I fling my hands up as if the bear's holding a gun on me. My heart is going so fast I think I might pass out, but I'm too distracted by Jake's display. "Aren't we supposed to curl into a ball?"

"Not with black bears." Jake yells at the bear again. "Make yourself look big and intimidating. These bears aren't after a fight." He stamps his foot again. "Go on! Argh!"

I copy him, sort of. My legs are shaking so badly, I'm surprised I'm not falling over.

The bear is huge. If Jake's wrong and it decides to attack, there's no way we'll survive those vicious claws, those teeth. Its weight alone would crush us.

"Go," I whisper. "Please, go!" I wave my arms, rising to my tiptoes and trying to look as tall as possible.

The bear's ear twitches and after a moment, it drops to all fours.

"Is it gonna charge?" I jump toward Jake, snatching his jacket sleeve and fisting the material.

"It's okay." Jake puffs, his wide blue eyes staring the bear down.

After a gruff headshake, the beast sniffs the shelter entrance one more time before turning and lumbering off.

As soon as it's out of sight, I crumple. Jake catches me before my butt hits the dirt, slowing my descent.

"Are you okay?" He brushes the hair off my face.

I glance up at him and rasp, "Okay." My nod becomes less erratic as my heart rate reduces to within the realms of normal. "I can't believe that just happened."

"I'm sorry." Jake cringes, turning to scowl at his backpack. "I wasn't thinking straight last night. I should have tied my bag up in a tree away from us or something. We're in the wilderness. Of course we should be locking up our food! Idiot," he mutters to himself, shaking his head so hard, his dirty-blond locks flop across his forehead.

"Hey, it's okay. Don't beat yourself up. You totally saved us from that bear."

He nods but is still frowning. "I shouldn't have had to. I won't make that mistake with the food again. I promise." He glances down at me, his blue eyes so sincere. I love that look on him; it makes my heart shift into funny shapes, sends tingles through my chest. Delicious tingles that make me want to smile.

If we were anywhere else right now, I would.

But I'm still kind of reeling over being face-to-face with a big-ass bear.

"We're good, though." He nods again, obviously talking to himself. "We're alive. We handled it, and now we can keep moving."

"Keep moving," I murmur, then gasp. "What? You mean out there?" I point to where the bear just stood.

He blinks and looks at me. "Well, yeah. We can't stay here. The bear isn't after us."

"He wants our food." I frown, gazing past Jake's arm to double-check the animal's not lumbering back for a second attempt.

"He won't want to fight us for it, though. We scared him off."

I bite my lip, still unsure.

Jake's probably right. I don't know huge amounts about wildlife, but his superhero is Bear Grylls. If anyone's gonna know, it'll be him.

Glancing into his eyes, I find my faith in that blue gaze and let him help me back to my feet.

He shoulders the pack, clipping it around his waist. He notices me watching him, and his mouth curls at the edges.

I try to smile back but can't.

I hover near the entrance, checking for noises and movement in the forest around us. All seems quiet, but I don't quite trust it.

"Do you need to pee or anything?" Jake glances over his shoulder as he jumps out of the shelter.

"Um." My cheeks flare with color as I nod and admit, "Yeah."

"Me too." He points to a thick crop of trees to his left. "I'll go this way and keep my back turned." His wink is kind of adorable, and I can't help smiling as he saunters off like black bears don't exist and we're not lost in the wilderness.

I creep around the back of the shelter, my body on full alert to the point I nearly can't pee. It takes a few deep breaths and a little self-talk to finally get going, and man, it's a relief. I didn't realize how busting I was.

Straightening myself out, I walk around to the front of the shelter. Jake's standing there, studying his compass. The morning light filtering through the trees bathes him in a soft glow that illuminates the ends of his hair and the edges of his face.

He hasn't noticed my approach, so I stay still, drinking him in for a moment. I've quietly studied him so many times in the past, but never like this. Never so brazenly. So unchecked. It's just the two of us out here. No one's watching me. Judging me. I can openly stare and... and feel it.

He's so good-looking. And smart. And kind.

And he played my game last night.

And he protected me from a bear. He knew exactly what to do.

Jake glances up, a smile curling his lips when he spots me. "You ready to go?"

"Yeah." The word comes out as a flushed whisper.

He doesn't seem to notice as he spins and starts leading us south again.

"There's got to be water around here somewhere, so keep an ear out for the sound of a river or something."

I step up right behind him, following his steps and straining to take in the noises around me.

This is all so foreign and frightening. The tragedy and terror of this weekend has stolen what could be something magical. I'm in the middle of nowhere, nature around me on all sides. It's just the forest and me and Jake. My eyes should be open with wonder. This weekend was supposed to be something beautiful and awe-inspiring. Death has annihilated that dream, turned the landscape dark and sinister.

Listen for a river, Carmen.

But I can't.

A bloody knife pierces my vision. It's horrific and unexpected, sending a shudder through me.

Alejandro. My heart weeps for the loss. My logic starts drowning, swelling the ever-present anxiety lurking in my stomach.

Ademir. Was his blood smeared on the dirt around him? Did the explosion rip his limbs from his body, mar his handsome face? Did he die slowly in pain, or did his heart stop beating as the force of the blast flung him through the air?

The weight in my chest is too heavy. Something is squeezing my lungs. My heart is thundering. Painful images tear through me like a horror movie on repeat.

I can't breathe.

My chest hurts!

Panic sizzles the edges of my brain. *Shit! I'm going to lose it!*

Stop it, Carmen! Keep it together!

You can't think about them right now. You have to survive.

For Donita.

For Jake. Don't put him through one of your panic attacks. Just breathe, dammit!

Remember what the shrink said. Focus on something else. Take control. Be present.

Take in the sounds around you! Work out the noises. Focus on just that.

I snatch the last of my rationale and cling to it.

Noises around me.

Inhale. Exhale.

The noises around me.

Inhale.

Our crunching feet.

Exhale.

Hiking boots on dry sticks and dead pine needles.

Inhale.

A bird flying.

Exhale

Wings fluttering.

As I practice the art of calming down, my senses become attuned to the world around me. I start to hear birds calling to each other—a soft twitter, a sharp little shout. The gentle sway of trees above me, the whistle of wind as it plays with pine needles.

My heart rate slows, the weight on my chest easing up.

Yes! I'm doing it! I'm beating this one.

Triumph skirts through me, and I smile at the scampering of squirrels across branches.

Inhaling a full breath, I hold it for a moment, then let it whistle out my nose.

Wait. Do I hear a faint rush of water in the distance?

I tip my head, not wanting to say anything until I'm totally sure. But my strain to hear the sweet lullaby of a river is interrupted by an ugly sound that doesn't belong here.

Gunshot!

I flinch, ducking my shoulders and spinning around with a gasp. The remnants of the sound seem to echo and pulse in the air, the animals suddenly falling silent. It's like the Earth goes still, holding its breath, waiting for that moment when it's safe to move again.

"Don't stop." Jake snatches my hand and pulls me after him.

I'm back to crashing feet and erratic breathing.

"Where did that come from?" I wriggle my hand free of his grasp so I can pump my arms and run faster.

"Not sure." Jake whips back to look at me. "Behind us, maybe. It's hard to tell."

He veers right, around a big tree, and I follow him, jumping over a fallen trunk and skidding down the other side.

Jake turns back to help me. "You good?"

"Yeah. Just go. Go!"

He takes off, and I keep up with him. No more shots

are fired, but we're like startled horses, trying to put as much distance between us and Alejandro's killers.

It's got to be them, right?

Or maybe it's hunters. Someone who could help us.

"I think I hear water!" Jake yells before I have time to verbalize my thoughts.

"Hey, do you think—" I burst through the brush he's just crashed through and shriek as the ground I was expecting to feel has abandoned me.

Stepping onto a pile of nothing, my body drops like a stone.

"Ahh!" I scream, the sound swallowed as I hit the icy water and am immediately sucked under.

Sharp needles pierce my exposed skin, stealing my breath as I scramble back to the surface.

I breach the top, the water pulling me swiftly away from the rocks.

"Jake!"

I kick hard, my arms flailing as my chin dips below the surface. I get a mouthful of water and have to lurch up, scrambling to suck in a lungful of air.

Coughing and spluttering, I try to swim against the swift current, but don't have a shot.

I'm moving too fast.

Where's Jake?

"Jake!" I scream his name again and spot him just before going under.

My boots are like cast iron as I struggle to propel myself back to the top. My head pops above the surface, and I see Jake clinging to a rock on the other side of the river.

"Carmen!"

I fight the current, angling my body so I can swim across the river. My limbs tire quickly, my waterlogged clothes and numbing fear working against me.

How am I going to make it across to him?

I don't know if I have the strength to reach him.

As if proving me right, my body drops below the surface once again.

25

IT'S EASY TO FORGET

I'M NOT GOING to let her drown.

I start swimming before I can think better of it, fighting against the weight of my backpack, the drag of my hiking boots.

I have to reach her.

It's all I can think about as I ignore my burning muscles.

Her head pops back up, closer to me this time, and I surge forward. She starts powering across to me.

Yes! Swim hard, Carmen. Reach me!

As if pulled by magnets, we miraculously draw closer. The second her arm brushes past mine, I snatch it, hauling her to my side. Clinging to her waist, I lock her against me, and we ride the river together. We're at the current's mercy, and I can tell we're not riding a friendly river. We're going to hit rapids soon—bigger, scarier, more brutal than the ones we're already coursing along on.

"Kick," I rasp, directing Carmen toward the edge.

We need to grab a rock, a branch, something to haul us out of here.

"There!" Carmen gasps, spluttering water out of her mouth. "Over there!"

I whip a look left and spot the branch hanging over the river. It looks thick enough to hold us, but at the speed we're going, I'll be lucky to catch it.

Kicking hard, we steer toward it, and I snatch the tree as soon as I'm close enough. The rough bark cuts into my freezing skin, but I cling tight. The water protests my decision, rushing past us and trying to loosen my grip. I wish I was stronger. I wish I was Brody. He'd probably grunt and be able to haul both him and Carmen out of the water in one easy move.

Clinging with aching fingers, I will my determination to be enough.

We're not being pulled down these rapids. We will survive.

Carmen reaches up and grabs onto the branch as well, taking some of the weight I was trying to bear. With a little grunt, she starts shifting us toward the rocky bank.

I kick with her. It's exhausting work, but we huff, puff, and pull ourselves out of the river, finally reaching safety and collapsing. Coughing out the water I accidentally sucked in, I fight my burning lungs. Carmen's hacking beside me, sucking in mouthfuls of air and then coughing all over again.

I crawl toward her, lightly patting her back until she's breathing steadily again.

A cool air whistles over us, making the cold water we've just been dumped in feel icy. I shiver and clench my jaw. My teeth want to chatter.

Carmen rolls over, blinking water from her eyes and staring at me. Droplets run down her face like rain. Her hair is plastered to her cheek, and her lips are just a little blue as they tremble and shake from the cold.

I need to get her warm.

But all I can do is stare at her... the same way she's staring at me.

Her large brown eyes are wide, and I can tell what she's thinking.

We could have just drowned.

The thought makes us move in unison, and before I know what's happening, she's in my arms, her lips pressed against mine in a kiss that's all passion and no thought.

Her mouth... those sultry, beautiful lips I have dreamed about so many times before... I'm finally touching them, tasting them. They're as perfect as I thought they'd be. Soft and supple. The cold from the river water is a heady contrast to the warmth of her tongue.

Her tongue. It just brushed against mine.

My heart spikes, the sensation addictive.

I cup the back of her head, deepening the kiss like it's the only thing I was born to do. Pulling her on top of me, I run my hand over her wet clothes, the sound of our saturated bodies a unique melody to the tango of our lips.

Her soft moan adds another layer to this intoxicating dancing, and I fist the back of her shirt, loving her weight on me, the drips of water that are running from her face onto mine. I swear, I could do this all freaking day.

I know we're cold and we need to move away from the river's edge, but I can't stop what's happening right now.

My tongue sweeps into Carmen's mouth once more, and a small murmur of pleasure rumbles in my throat.

That's when she pulls away.

With a little gasp, she sits back, her eyes wide with realization.

"What am I doing?" she whispers, scrambling off me, her chest heaving as she runs shaking hands over her face. "I'm sorry."

And then she bolts.

Sprinting into the forest, she disappears while I'm still trying to get blood to my brain and figure out what the hell is going on.

"Wait!" It's an effort to move away from that euphoria, but I manage to clamber to my feet and run after her. "Carmen, stop!"

I track the sound of running feet and have to call out two more times before she finally goes still. I find her in a small clearing, her hand resting over her mouth while her other arm is curled around her waist. Her clothes stick to her in wrinkles and clumps. Her curvy figure is on full display as the material clings to all the right places.

I run my eyes over her body, taking a moment to catch my breath.

"Hey." Knowing better than to touch her, I soften my tone, moving around in order to see her face better.

Her wide brown gaze brushes over me before she looks to the ground. "I'm sorry. You must think I'm this awful person. This… cheater," she ends with a whisper.

I let out a small laugh and shake my head. "I'm pretty sure I wasn't thinking about Hector when we were kissing just then. In fact, I'm certain the world ceased to exist for a minute."

A tiny smile tugs at her lips, but she fights it off, looking up at me with the disappointing truth. "I have a boyfriend." Her expression crumples into what looks like confusion. Or maybe it's something else.

The way she said *boyfriend* makes me wonder how much she actually wants to have one right now.

I don't know what it is. There's just this uncertain flicker in her eyes.

"Why?" I have to ask. "What is it about Hector that makes you stay? He treated you like shit yesterday, and the night before." I huff, unable to hide my frustration over the whole thing. I don't mean for it to happen, but I guess it's months' worth of angst finally breaking through. "I just don't get it. He's so wrong for you, yet you stay."

I scrub a hand down my face and turn my back to her, not really sure I want the answer.

Resting my hands on my hips, I contemplate cutting

this conversation short. Is it really any of my business? So we made out after a near-death experience. With adrenaline flowing through us the way it has been, there's probably some scientific explanation for our actions.

Well, on her part anyway.

I'd kiss her any day.

Not that she knows that.

I close my eyes, dipping my chin and wondering if now is the right time to finally say it.

But... a man's been killed. Murdered. We're on the run for our lives. It's hardly the most appropriate place to be doing this.

And she has a boyfriend.

I clench my jaw, unsure whether to spin around or simply mumble over my shoulder that we should keep walking. We need to move, get warm. We need to—

A soft sniff makes me whip back around. Carmen's perched on a fallen tree trunk, her mouth forming a wonky line as she sits there shivering and obviously fighting tears.

"I'm sorry," I quickly say, closing the space between us and crouching at her feet. "Please don't cry, I didn't—" I wince and start rubbing her arms. "Let's just get you warm and—"

"It's not you. It's me." Her face fills with anguish. "I'm crying because of me."

I let her go, shaking my head in confusion.

"You're right to ask me about Hector and why I stay. He's wrong for me. I know he is, but..." She closes her eyes, releasing a few tears. Her chin bunches, and she sucks in another breath; then her face crumples in a look of disgust. "If I tell you the real reason, you're never gonna look at me the same." She jolts up and moves away from me, slashing at her tears and shaking her head. "You'll think I'm this weak, pathetic..." She sucks in a breath, shaking her head some more.

"What do you mean?" I stand, following her with my eyes.

After a long beat, she sniffs and looks over her shoulder.

Her beautiful gaze connects with mine, and I'm locked still, waiting for the big reveal. I don't know what she's about to say, but whatever it is... I won't change my mind about her. I've been crushing on her for way too long.

I should tell her that.

I open my mouth, but she speaks before I can.

"My brother," she whispers, turning to face me. She shudders and hugs herself, squeezing her biceps until her knuckles turn white.

I want to pry her fingers loose so she doesn't hurt herself, but I'm not sure if I should get that close right now.

Bobbing her head, she looks into the forest and softly admits, "I don't talk about him very often, because... it hurts too much."

My stomach plummets, and I think I already know my answer, but I have to ask anyway. "What happened?"

"He... he died. He was deployed two years ago, and... he never came home. IED." Her voice fades but then finds its strength again after another deep breath. "I didn't tell anyone. I just wanted Stanford to be a new start, and I made Hector swear he'd keep it quiet." She looks down, and I so badly want to go to her, wrap my arms around her.

I know this pain.

I've lived it.

Do I have the guts to tell her?

But then she'll ask questions. Carmen's curious. It's one of the things I love most about her. She loves to learn, to understand, to fully comprehend. She'll want to know my story.

A sharp pain lodges behind my rib cage. It's an uncomfortable panic that holds me silent.

"Hector used to be friends with my brother. In high school. He'd hang out with my family a lot, and he was really there for me... after... after..." She works her jaw to the side. It's trembling. Whether it's from cold or emotion, I'm not sure, but I need to get her warm.

I nearly interrupt and put practicality in the front seat, but she starts talking again, looking almost embarrassed as she admits, "We got together the summer after Ademir died, and my parents were just so happy. He was like this balm to ease the pain. Life didn't have to be miserable all the time. There was joy still. Hector made my mom smile, and my dad started to interact again." Her nose wrinkles. "But after a while, I realized that Hector might not be the one. The problem was, if I broke up with him, it would destroy my parents. They adore him. They treat him like a son, and I'm pretty sure they're expecting us to get married after I graduate." Her brown eyes grow wide as she stares at the ground, panic flickering over her expression. "I don't want to hurt them, so I've just kept playing along." She starts blinking, her swallow thick and audible as her knuckles turn even whiter from gripping so hard. "I thought I could do it. I figured it'd be okay. Hector's not a bad person. He's a little unaware sometimes, but he was enough..." Her eyes slowly track to mine, and the look on her face turns the whole world still. "Until I met you."

And yeah, breathing is so off the table right now.

Is she saying what I think she's saying?

Me?

She's into me.

She wants me.

It's hard to fight my smile as I carefully step toward her.

Reaching for her hand, I wait until her fingers are resting in mine before saying what needs to be said. "You're not pathetic or weak. You've been trying to do the right thing for everybody else. That actually shows strength."

Her lips quiver with a smile, a dimple coming to life on her cheek when she ducks her head in that shy way of hers.

"But, Carmen, you can't forfeit the rest of your life for—"

"I know." She starts nodding. "I know. And I've been trying to find the courage to end it. I have. I really have." She scoffs. "His behavior on this trip has been extremely helpful, but I think he was just jealous. He could sense whatever this is between us, and it's the first time he's really gotten to see it. I didn't realize we were so obvious, because we've never been anything more than friends, but... maybe I've been lying to myself." Her voice trails off, her cheeks flushing with a pretty heat. "The other night, at camp, I kind of told Hector that I didn't want to be with him anymore." She cringes.

"I heard you guys arguing, but I didn't know you were breaking up with him."

"Well, I was kind of trying to, but he refused to talk about it, so I guess we're not officially over. Except that we are." She nods like she's confirming this with herself. "We have to be. I can't keep lying to everybody. If we make it out of this, I need a fresh start. A new beginning." A smile toys with her lips as she looks up and catches my eye.

A new beginning.

With me.

She wants to be with me.

I brush my fingers down her cheek, resting them on the pulse in her neck. It's quick, just like mine. Does her heart want to burst? Is she fighting the heady tingle that's buzzing in my brain and firing down to my stomach?

Her nose wrinkles, her face crumpling for a second. "I guess I'll have to find a way to tell my parents. That's the part that scares me most."

"You can do it," I whisper and smile. "Carmen, you're the most amazing woman. You can do anything."

She shakes her head, obviously not believing me.

"I'll fight for you. With you. Whatever you need. I can be your man."

Her smile is radiant when she looks up, and she takes a small step closer. "You want to be my man?"

"For so long." I grin, my face suddenly on fire. "Carmen, you're... you're the only girl I've ever felt this way about. But I couldn't do anything because you were with Hector. So I tried to pretend like being your friend was enough."

"But it's not," she whispers.

"I love being your friend, but I want more. And maybe I should have told you sooner."

She shakes her head, running her hand around the back of my neck and stepping into my space. As her lips find their home against mine, it's easy to forget that we're standing in a vast wilderness, lost, wet, cold, and running from a pack of crazies.

It's easy to forget because only two people exist right now—me and the only girl I've ever truly wanted.

26

THERE ONE MINUTE, GONE
THE NEXT

Carmen

JAKE'S ARMS wrap around my waist, suctioning us together. It's easy to forget about the chill sweeping over me when our lips are locked together this way. He's a really good kisser. His tongue is tentative and sweet, teasing mine as we shift our heads and deepen the kiss in a new way.

I can't believe I'm actually doing this.

I've never let myself truly entertain the thought of being with Jake in this way, but now that I am, it's obliterating everything else. We're meant to be together. As I run my fingers into his hair and fist the wet clumps, I can feel it right through my center. I was born to kiss this man.

This friend. This wonderful person who I've cared about for so long.

Jake's hands roam my back, running up my spine and pressing us even closer together.

Yes, this is so freaking right.

I've never experienced anything like it before. Why did I wait so long? Fear's been holding me hostage, keeping me in a relationship that was dehydrating my soul. Jake's words, his lips, his body are reviving it again, pouring fresh spring water into the crevices and giving me the courage to do what I need to.

It's going to be tough, but I can do it. I have to tell my parents the truth. And no matter how they respond, at least I know Jake will be waiting in the wings to hold me and remind me why this pain is such a small sacrifice.

We have to get out of this forest.

We have to survive so I can finally start living the life I want.

The thought jolts me and I pull out of the kiss, clutching Jake's arms and forcing us apart.

"What?" he whispers. His disappointment is so freaking cute.

I grin, my teeth chattering as the cold river water starts to seep into my core.

"K-kissing won't get us dry. We have to survive this and keep moving. It's time to get on with m-my life. To save Donita. To do the right thing."

Jake smiles, his eyes shining with pride, his body shaking with the cold as well. "Come on." He takes my hand and starts looking around. "Let's find some shelter and get you out of those clothes."

"Excuse me?" I jerk my hand out of his, about to tell him that yes, I really like him, but that doesn't mean I'm ready to—

He smiles and shakes his head, taking my hand and lightly kissing my knuckles.

"Not that." He tips his head and wiggles his eyebrows. "Although that would be amazing, I just mean we need to get dry. Warm. Catching hypothermia won't help us get out of here. And staying in these wet clothes is a big no-no."

I blush, embarrassed by my indignant assumption.

"Trust me." He winks and starts pulling me into the forest. "I've got some dry clothes we can share."

I glance at his sodden pack and wonder if he's being overly hopeful.

"Let's collect some firewood as we walk."

"But... a fire?"

"We have to get warm. I know it's a risk, but hopefully with the river between us, we've scored ourselves some time. We'll build it small and stamp it out as soon as we're dry."

I nod, understanding his logic, and then follow his instructions. Within twenty minutes, we've collected firewood, found shelter within a thick clump of trees, and built a small fire.

I hold my hands up to the feeble flame and wonder how quickly it'll take to grow. Moving around has been good, but I'm still freezing.

"Here." Jake pulls a plastic bag out of his pack. "Start taking your clothes off and ring them out. We'll hang them out to dry on those branches over there."

Pulling a dry shirt and pants out of the bag, he hands me the shirt and then turns away so I can get changed in private.

That's so sweet. He's always so respectful. I love that about him.

Peeling off my wet clothes, I ring them out, hanging them over low-lying branches and trying not to peek at Jake.

I'm down to my underwear when I lose the fight and have to glance behind me. He's pulling on his dry pants, and I get a microsecond flash of his curved butt before he secures the pants around his waist. My eyes linger on his bare back, mesmerized by the way his sinewy muscles move while hanging his wet clothes over branches.

"Is it safe to turn around?" he asks.

My eyes bulge, and I quickly whip back. "Just a second." Unclasping my wet bra, I hang that up and pull his dry shirt over me. It only just reaches past my butt, so I decide to leave my underwear on, even though it's wet and uncomfortable.

Spinning around, I take one more moment of appreciation before rasping, "Okay."

Jake turns, drinking me in, his lips rising with a slow, appreciative smile. "I like my clothes on you."

It's impossible not to blush as I step toward the fire and find a perch on a rock nearby. The hard, cold stone digs into my butt, and I shift to get a little more comfortable.

Jake sits beside me, pulling out some trail mix and pouring a little into my palm.

"Sorry, we need to ration."

"That's okay." I nibble at the nuts, raisins, dried cranberries, and dark chocolate chips.

"After this, I'll head back to the river and see if I can reach down and refill my water bottle."

"Be careful." My eyes bulge.

"I will." He smiles around his mouthful of food. "We have to keep hydrated, though. The body can go three minutes without air, three days without water, and three weeks without food. I don't want us testing that theory."

I grin and bite into a cashew while Jake unpacks his bag and lays things out to dry. He's got so much stuff in there—a first aid kit, pocketknife, a multi-tool of some sort, compass, flashlight.

"Wow, you really are a survival expert."

He shrugs. "I'm not as prepared as I should have been. A shelter and GPS would have been handy, but I didn't think we'd be in this situation, so I just kept the essentials on hand."

"That's a lot of essentials."

He grins. "Well, I love this kind of thing."

"But why'd you have it on you while filming?" I tip my head, curious at his overpreparation. I mean, I'm grateful for it, but a little perplexed. We were just filming in the forest.

Jake's smile is shy as he runs a hand through his

floppy hair and rubs the back of his neck. "I like to be prepared. It makes me feel... like I can handle anything." His voice trails off, and I nearly miss the last part.

There's a tightness to his expression that has me wondering if there's more to what he's saying. Like this need to be prepared has a deeper meaning.

Has he had to survive something harrowing the way I have?

The loss of a family member?

Foster homes. He lost his parents. Maybe that's it. Shifting from one place to another, having to survive.

Or maybe he experienced something else as a kid that freaked him out and now he has to be prepared to feel safe?

Stop psychoanalyzing him and just be grateful he is this way. You're in a dry shirt right now!

I finish the trail mix and take a few sips of water before Jake heads off to refill the bottle. I offer to go with him so he doesn't fall in, but he shakes his head.

"Stay by the fire. Keep warm. I promise I'll be careful." He winks and walks away.

As he disappears into the trees, I'm taken out by visions of Ademir.

"You look after yourself, little sis." He pulled me into a tight hug, and I clung to his shoulders.

I was proud of him, yet hating him at the same time.

Why'd he have to join the army?

Why'd he have to leave us?

He let me go and gazed down at me with a sweet smile. "You're my favorite person."

I couldn't stop my grin. "And you're mine."

"Don't go falling for a douchebag while I'm not around to watch your back."

"Yes, sir." I saluted him.

His face flickered with a quick emotion I couldn't quite capture, and then he gave me one more tight squeeze before walking away. Mom wrapped her arm around my waist as we stood in a clump waving him off.

I didn't know it was the last time I was ever going to see him.

If I had, I would have held on a little tighter. I wouldn't have wasted a second of emotion resenting him for leaving. I would have told him how much he meant to me and how much I'd miss him.

I wouldn't have let him just walk away like that.

I blink, tears scorching my throat as a wave of panic fires through me.

Jake. I shouldn't have let him go alone. What if he falls in? What if he gets hurt?

I can't handle that.

I can't be alone.

Bolting from my spot, I'm getting ready to race into the forest after him, but then he appears.

"Are you okay?" His face flickers with concern, and I have to check myself, wondering what my own expression is doing.

Forcing a smile, I let out a little laugh and shake my head. "Just wondering if I should have gone with you."

His smile is affectionate as he steps around the fire and wraps his arm around my shoulders. Kissing the side of my head, he gives me a squeeze. "I promised I'd be careful." He holds out his drink bottle. "The tablet's already dissolved. It's safe to drink."

I nod and gulp down some icy mouthfuls, grateful for the fluid.

Plunking back down on my rock, I drink a little more, then hold the bottle while Jake secures the SD card in his dry pants. There's a small zipper compartment hidden on the side, and he tucks it safely away, patting it and giving me a serious nod.

Without a word, he's telling me we're going to make it.

But how does he really know?

Life is way too unpredictable.

It can end in a moment. It can change in a heartbeat.

Ademir was there beside me, telling me I'm his favorite person, and then he was gone.

It was so sudden. So fast.

He was alive one afternoon, and then he was dead.

Just like Alejandro. The expression on his bloodied face before he died flashes through me, and it suddenly hurts to breathe.

27

KEEP MOVING. STAY CALM.

"THEY'RE NOT GOING to give up looking for us, are they?" Carmen's voice is quiet and out of the blue. I glance at her face, noticing how pale and pinched it is.

Just stay calm, man. Be the voice of reason.

I secure the water bottle back in my pack and start checking to see if things are dry enough to put away. That gunshot is still ringing in the back of my mind, and even though we made it across the river, those guys could be anywhere.

A muscle in my jaw twitches as I try to form a decent reply.

The truth, Jake. Just go with the truth.

"If I was them, I wouldn't stop. They saw me filming, and if we make it out of here, they could end up in jail for a really long time."

Carmen's brown eyes grow wide, and her head starts bobbing. I didn't realize how much of a nervous tick that was, but this trip is highlighting so many things about her. New little nuances to fall in love with.

"We can't surrender." I keep my voice soft but firm. Standing up, I uncap the water bottle and empty the contents over the fire. "I doubt they just want the footage. We're witnesses."

"And if they can kill Alejandro like that, they won't hesitate to end us as well." Her voice trips and trembles, and I stop what I'm doing.

Moving to her side, I crouch beside her and run my hand down her back.

"Do you think Hector and Lenny made it?"

I pause, not wanting to be flippant with my reply, but what can I honestly say?

"I hope so." I nod. "They can alert the authorities. Send help."

"If they can find us." Carmen starts to blink, and I see the edges of panic curling over her again. Her skin is paler than it was a moment ago.

Moving to cup her face in my hands, I gently force her to look at me. "Breathe."

"I can't."

"Yes you can. You can breathe, and you can stop thinking for a second."

She tries to shake her head, but I'm holding her securely.

"Breathe, Carmen."

She sucks in a short, stiff breath.

"Stop thinking about it."

Squeezing her eyes shut, she takes in another few breaths before finally releasing it all on a shudder and leaning forward to rest her head on my shoulder.

"I never used to be this bad." Her voice trembles. "But then Ademir got deployed, and I just felt scared all the time. When we found out he'd died, it was like all my fear was justified, and I couldn't logically talk myself out of it. I've learned some management techniques, but they don't always work. I'm trying. I'm really trying." She whimpers.

My heart curls in pain for her. I so want to make this better. To squeeze the life out of her fear and give her hope again.

Alejandro's death won't be helping. Shit, she's probably reliving this past pain all over again.

What can I say to make this better?

Nothing. You just have to move. To do. Be practical.

That's my usual MO—cut off emotion and just get doing.

But something holds me still, and before I know what I'm saying, the words are coming out of me. "I know what it's like to lose. I lost my grandpa, who was the best person in the world. And then my brothers all left me, one by one, and I—" Anger cuts off my voice.

Carmen sits up, her surprised expression making me wish I'd kept my mouth shut.

With a sharp shake of my head, I run my hand up and down her arm. "We can't rely on anybody but us, okay? But we can do this. I won't let you down. I won't leave you. You don't have to be afraid."

She stares at me, lightly brushing her fingers down my cheek with a look that makes me want to kiss her... or maybe run away.

She's going to undo me.

I can feel it. That kind gaze of hers wants to delve inside my soul.

Standing to my feet, I rest my hands on my hips and get back to the safety of logic.

"We should probably get moving. Are you feeling dry enough? Warm enough?" I brush past her to check on the clothes hanging from branches. "Your pants are still damp, but they're drier than before. Why don't we just get dressed and hike a little more while we've got daylight."

She doesn't say anything, just looks at me with those gentle brown eyes.

It's a little unnerving, but eventually she bobs her head. "Okay."

Relief pulses through me in a thick beat, and I nod, grateful we can avoid the pain from my past for just a little longer. Although I've got a feeling this isn't the end.

If I want to be with Carmen, then I need to tell her everything.

Everything? Forget it!

You've got to give her more than what you have, man. And you know it.

Shaking the thought away, I start organizing my stuff, pulling on my damp shirt and packing up the rest of the gear before getting more river water and dousing the fire again. I add some dirt and poke the ashes with a stick to make sure the fire's completely cool and extinguished.

Once Carmen finishes lacing her boots, I force a smile and ask, "You ready?"

She nods, and I check the compass one more time before taking her hand and heading south.

We keep the river on our right. The soft roar in the distance is almost comforting as we hike through the vast wilderness. We spot deer, the tail end of a moose, and manage to avoid another black bear before finally coming to rest miles from where we started.

Carmen flops against a tree, running a hand over her face and finally admitting, "I'm sorry. I can't go any farther."

"Yeah, that's cool." I glance at my watch, figuring late afternoon is a good time to stop. "I'll start looking for a shelter."

She nods, not saying anything.

We didn't speak much as we walked today. I pointed out things in nature and that led to the odd discussion, but then we settled into silence again, and that worked too.

There's a cloud hovering over us—it's gray and ominous, filled with droplets of truth that I don't want to unleash, but I can't help feeling that I'm going to have to eventually. Carmen's not blind. Hell, she's one of the smartest people I know, and there's not a chance she didn't pick up on the emotion roaring through me when I mentioned my brothers.

She'll want to know more, and can I honestly hold back from telling her?

My insides simmer as we silently prepare a shelter in the small clearing we've found. I remember to hide my bag away from where we'll be resting, climbing a tree and wedging it into a V made from a branch and trunk. Hopefully any bears will stay clear of us tonight and the small wildlife won't be smart enough to unzip my pack. I hate having it so far away—makes me feel vulnerable somehow —but it's better that than facing a big black bear again.

I hike back to our spot, surveying the surroundings and hoping we'll be safe enough. The large trees are centurions, blocking us from the elements on all sides. There's nothing over our heads, but the days have been mercifully clear, so fingers crossed we'll stay dry as we sleep.

If we can sleep.

My muscles are wound tight as I split a granola bar in half and pass Carmen her portion. I'm so freaking hungry, but I don't want to admit it. There's nothing we can do about a food source right now, and we've only got a little trail mix and two bars left. Our energy is waning with every passing hour.

We have to make it out of the forest tomorrow. I don't know how we're gonna do it, but there's gotta be a way.

Carmen scrunches up the wrapper and tucks it into the pocket of her jacket. I watch her long fingers, kind of awed by how she can make even that look graceful.

Flicking her braid behind her back, she looks at me, a soft smile curling her lips as she moves and takes a seat right beside me.

I automatically lift my arm over her and pull her against me. It's weird how this is so new yet feels so natural.

She nestles the top of her head into the crook of my neck, and we let the noises of nature settle around us. It's kind of peaceful in a way. Makes it easy to forget the harsh realities and pretend like we're just two lovebirds on a camping trip.

"How'd your grandpa die?" Carmen whispers.

The question's like a slap to the face, but I absorb it, knowing it was coming.

Rubbing my thumb over her shoulder, I look up at the sky, homing in on the deep blue hue that will soon be dotted with stars and wondering how much to say. I haven't spoken about Grandpa in years. It hurts too much.

But she told me about her brother, so it's only fair that I tell her about the world's best person.

28

BITTERNESS

Carmen

HE TAKES A MOMENT TO ANSWER, and I wonder if I've crossed a line I shouldn't have.

But the questions have been swirling around my mind all day, and now that we've finally stopped and the world has gone quiet for a moment, I want to ask.

I thought it was right, but now—

"He was killed," Jake rasps. "By my father."

"What?" I try to shift away so I can look at his face, but he tightens his hold.

I relax against him, and he starts talking again.

"My father was a... a drunk. When my mother died of cancer, Grandpa Ray showed up and snuck us away to his ranch in Montana." Jake's voice breaks, and it's the most emotional I've ever heard him. He's always so in control and collected, but right now he sounds like he's about to cry. "We lived there for about eight years. And my dad had no idea where we were. I don't even know how he found out, but he showed up one night. He was out of his mind with rage, and he went after one of my brothers. Grandpa stepped in, and he got pushed." Jake bites his lips together, and I wait for more, but he doesn't say anything.

I have to assume he hit his head or landed on something if that's the reason he died.

I'm desperate to ask for more details, but I'm not sure if I should. I can feel Jake's chest thundering, his fingers curling around my shoulder and gripping tight.

"Jake," I whisper. Lightly shaking him, I run my hand over his cheek and make him turn to look at me. "What happened?"

I've never seen Jake's eyes like this before. They're glassy and such a vibrant blue—swirling with unmasked pain. His forehead bunches. "Dad pushed him, and he landed on the stones around the fireplace. Michael and I took him to the hospital, but he didn't make it."

"And what about your dad?"

"He's dead." Jake's voice turns cold and clipped. He looks to the side. "It was self-defense. After pushing Grandpa, he tried to kill Deeks. Cooper did what he had to. He saved us."

"Is Cooper your brother too?"

Jake nods and sniffs. "The oldest one."

"Older brothers are the best," I rasp, trying to smile and lighten the moment.

Jake scoffs and shakes his head. "The only one I've ever been able to rely on is my youngest. Brody's always been there for me. We take care of each other."

"And the others?"

He clenches his jaw and lightly pushes my hand off his cheek. "They left. Cooper took off after Grandpa's funeral. Social services split us up. Brody and I went to foster care. Deeks and Michael were put in a group home." Snatching a thin stick off the ground, he snaps it with one hand and throws it over his shoulder.

I bite my bottom lip, wondering what to say, trying to find my courage.

As the silence stretches around us, I can sense Jake's tension and close my eyes, willing the words out of my mouth. "You said your brothers left you. I know you probably don't want to talk about it, but... what happened to Michael and Deeks?"

"They ran away. Left without a goodbye."

"When?"

"Before the first year was even up!" he snaps. "And now they just want back into my life, you know? Like nothing even happened!"

"What are you talking about?" I shift out of his arms so I can turn and see him properly.

He looks away, his fine features wrinkling as he scowls at the trees around us.

"Jake, have they tried to make contact with you again?"

With a stiff nod, he licks his lips and explains. "Years

of nothing, and then all of a sudden they swoop in expecting everything to be fine again. Brody's stoked. He's gone off to the ranch. The place Grandpa died." He turns to me with a look of pure anguish. "He's gone to recover there like it's not a graveyard. Like the worst night of our lives didn't take place inside those walls." With a hard sniff, he shakes his head. "They act like the pain never existed, like it was fine that they just abandoned us. They're ready now, so it's all good for them!"

"What have they been doing?"

"I don't know." Jake shrugs. "I don't care."

I'm not used to this brittle tone. Jake's always so sweet and kind. I don't recognize this bitterness in him. It's harsh and unforgiving.

It hurts me, because I can see how much it hurts him.

I wish I could help him.

He glances at me, probably wondering why I'm not saying anything. Does he want me to side with him and start ranting about how his brothers have no right to show back up in his life again?

I can't say that.

I'd do anything to see Ademir one more time, even if he had hurt me. At least I think I would. I'd want to at least hear him out.

"You don't... you don't want to find out where your brothers have been? They've obviously sought you out for a reason."

"I don't care," Jake murmurs. "They left without a word. That's not love."

"It sounds like desperation."

He throws me a sharp frown.

I try to soften it with a smile. Gently touching his face, I tip my head and whisper, "You don't know their story. Maybe they had to go."

He removes my hand and shuffles away from me. "Why are you standing up for them?"

"I'm not." I shake my head.

"It sure sounds like you are."

Biting my lips together, I dip my head and let the accusation hang. It's awkward, and any peace this quiet shelter might have offered has been obliterated.

29

SOME THINGS DON'T MAKE LOGICAL SENSE

Jake

I'VE RUINED IT.

This silence is a killer, and I'm not sure how to fix it.

I can't believe she's siding with Deeks and Michael. She says she's not, but why would she say that thing about desperation?

Like *I* wasn't desperate?

I was a scared fourteen-year-old going to public school for the first time, living with strangers. Okay, our first foster family was kind of nice, but they weren't Grandpa. I missed the ranch. I missed my brothers. I was heartsick over Cooper leaving, and then Michael and Deeks just… poof! They took off.

Hating this ugly space between Carmen and me, I swipe a hand across my mouth and shuffle back to her side. I won't sleep at all if we can't clear the air. It's not her fault my brothers are selfish pricks.

Glancing at her, I try to catch her eye, but she's still staring at the ground.

"Hey." I softly nudge her boot with mine.

Her lips curl into a half-hearted smile.

"So, um… biggest regret?"

"What?" She looks up with a confused frown.

I smile. "I don't know. I just miss the sound of your voice. I never get time alone with you; I finally do and I'm screwing it up. I just… asked a random question to get you talking again."

She studies me for a long, uncomfortable beat, but then her gaze grows warm with affection. "Biggest regret."

I cringe and she lets out a soft giggle, turning her body to lean against mine.

I wrap my arms around her front, resting my chin lightly on her cheek and relishing this feeling that I've wanted for so long.

"Not being honest about what I really want." Carmen's answer is quiet. "Man, if Ademir was still around, he would have kicked my butt for that." She lets out a breathy snicker. "I'd do anything to see him right now. If he was alive and he knew what kind of trouble we were in, he'd be the first one looking for us. He wouldn't have run the opposite direction like Hector did. He would have run toward me, made sure I was okay. He was the kind of guy who'd drop anything for me." She lets out an unsteady breath and whispers, "I was his favorite person."

There's something so sweet and heartbreaking about her words, her tone, the way her voice quivers. She and her brother must have been really close… the way I was with all of mine.

Which is why I've never been able to understand how they could leave that way.

"I used to think that about my brothers, that they'd do anything for me… that they'd always have my back." I regret the words the second they're out of my mouth.

What the hell am I doing? Circling around to this after only a few minutes? What is my problem?

"Well, that's a good thing, isn't it?"

"They abandoned me and Brody. They didn't have our backs. They left. How can I trust them again?"

"But they're trying to make it right." She squeezes my forearm. "They came to find you. They want to explain."

"Well, I'm not gonna let them. I can't forgive what they did. They abandoned us when we needed them most." I let the pain roll through me again, scorching all the raw spots. "It sucks that your brother died, but mine left by choice… and I hate them for it."

Carmen shifts around so she can look up at me. Hooking her legs over mine, she runs her knuckles down my jawline. My harsh words make her sad. Even in the dim light, I can see the sorrow in her gaze.

"I can see how much it hurts you." Her tone and gentle touch match perfectly and it does something to my heart.

My throat is so thick right now I can't speak, and my brain wants to rebel. Switch off! Don't feel! Don't let her unravel you!

But my heart...

She looks away from me, her long lashes catching my eye when she blinks.

Oh no! Have I made her cry again?

Stop doing that, you idiot!

I'm about to apologize, and then I'll change the subject and we can talk about something light and silly before drifting off to sleep, but she talks first.

"Do you know the story of the Good Samaritan?"

My forehead wrinkles. Where's she going with this?

I give her a fleeting glance before looking back at the growing darkness around us. It's a Bible story. I remember Grandpa telling it. He used to do that, would just randomly tell us a Bible story while we were eating dinner. I always found them so entertaining.

I scour my brain for the one about the Good Samaritan and eventually nod.

"Yeah, I know the one. It's about that guy on the road who gets beaten up and robbed. He's left to die in this ditch and gets looked over by the people who should have helped him—the priest and someone else just walk right past him, right?"

She nods, a smile curling the edges of her lips.

"And then the Samaritan comes along, and he's the unlikely hero of the story."

"Yeah, that's right." Carmen's dimples pop into place as her smile grows, but then her teeth catch her bottom lip and she looks away from me. "What do you think it means?"

"I don't know." I shrug, my jacket rustling. "Don't turn your back on people in need?"

"Well, yeah, but it means more."

My ears start to tingle for reasons I can't explain. I don't know what it is about her voice, but she has this siren-like effect on me sometimes. I'm mesmerized, caught by her beauty, her gentle tone, the elegant way she does everything.

Carmen snuggles her head into the crook of my neck and starts playing with the zipper of my jacket. "When Jesus told that story, the Samaritans were hated by the Jews. Those were turbulent times, and he was talking specifically to a Jewish man. See, a *good* Samaritan would have been an oxymoron to him. That concept didn't even exist for Jews. Samaritans were bad people, all of them. And the whole point of that story was to answer the question of 'Who is my neighbor?' You want me to love my neighbor—well, who is that?"

I can't move right now, so I stay perfectly still, soaking in her words and wondering why I'm so compelled to drink them all in.

"Jesus chose to make the unlikely hero a Samaritan, because he wanted to make his point loud and clear. We need to love *all* people, whether we share the same beliefs or not. Our neighbors aren't just the people we get along with, or the ones who are easy to love. Our neighbors are also the 'Samaritans.' The people we don't like. The people who hurt us and piss us off, the ones who are just easier to hate."

Jake scoffs. "We're supposed to love the people we hate?"

"We're supposed to love *everybody*, even the ones who do us wrong." She sits up, straddling my thighs so she can hold my face. "Jake, you have the power inside you to show love and compassion to anyone. But if you don't use it properly, that power turns bitter, and it becomes this infectious disease that robs you—makes your heart sick." She lays her hand over my heart. "Forgiveness, tolerance, trying to understand where others are coming from... that's your penicillin."

And now my eyes are tingling too. What is she doing to me?

Why is she telling me this Bible story?

And why is it affecting me so deeply?

"I'm not saying this to make you do anything, I just want you to think about it. Not for your brothers but for yourself." She drops a kiss on my lips. It's sweet and perfect... and not long enough. When she pulls away, she gives me the kind of smile that could melt a guy's heart before moving back to my side and resting against me. "I want you to be happy and free." She lays her hand over my heart again and lets the silence return.

It doesn't seem as thick and awkward as it did before, so I keep my lips shut, Carmen's words swirling in my brain like a tornado.

Forgive them for my sake?

That's a weird concept.

Love those you hate?

That's just bizarre.

So why am I not brushing this off as pure nonsense?

Why could Brody embrace Deeks and Michael without a second thought?

I think about my twin, picturing our lives together and how many times Brody was happier than me—upbeat, cheerful. He never carried burdens the way I did.

Was forgiveness his big secret?

I close my eyes, images of Grandpa returning to me with crystal clarity.

"There's no place for resentment, bitterness, or grudges in this house. I won't have it. You boys deserve a home that's fueled by love. After everything you've been through, I'll stop at nothing to make sure you get just that. So, Deeks and Cooper, you say you're sorry, and you forgive each other."

I can't even remember what that fight was about, but both my brothers' chests were heaving, their stances strong and obstinate.

"Life's too short for hate, boys." I mumble the words under my breath, seeing Grandpa saying them. At the time, I believed every word out of his mouth, and now I've got the girl of my dreams saying pretty much the same thing.

Is it too risky to start believing them?

Images of Michael and Deeks storm through me—the looks on their faces when I told them to leave me alone.

The pain in my chest starts up again. It's an irritating

niggle—or maybe it's a longing, kind of like homesickness.

The ranch. Can I seriously go back there?

Carmen lets out a soft sigh, her weight shifting on me like she's drifting to sleep in my arms. It's bizarre how the thing I've always wanted is happening in the worst situation.

Is life giving me some kind of wake-up call? Because it feels like being jolted by a defibrillator. It hurts, yet beneath that ache, there's this tiny spark of energy. Maybe something inside me does want to change... I just don't want it leading to more disappointment and heartache.

Survive this first, man. Then you can think about that.

Get Carmen home safe. Make sure Donita's okay. Get Alejandro the justice he deserves. After that, you can deal with both of your families' BS.

Pressing a kiss to the top of Carmen's head, I shuffle into a slightly more comfortable position and close my eyes. Yeah, I could get used to sleeping with her in my arms.

I have to make this my new normal.

Whatever it takes.

We're *going* to get out of this wilderness. We're *going* to get justice for Alejandro and freedom for Carmen. I need to make it so she can sleep in my arms whenever she wants to. And after that... then maybe I can think about the ranch. About a family I thought had abandoned me for good.

30

A KNIFE TO THE THROAT

Carmen

IT'S BEEN A RESTLESS NIGHT. As much as I love falling asleep on Jake's chest, it's hard to get comfortable. My neck and shoulders ache from the position and the cold. When a new day starts to register in my senses and I open my eyes, I'm aware that I'm now lying on my side. Something's digging into my hip, but all I can focus on is Jake's arm secured around my waist.

In spite of everything, a small smile curves the corners of my mouth and I close my eyes again, taking in every little sensation—the weight of his arm, the way his fingers are curled beneath my stomach, the feel of his body nestled behind me, his legs tucked up beneath my knees. We're like two puzzle pieces that fit perfectly together.

Why?

Why did I wait so long?

Why has it taken a life-or-death moment to act on what I've been feeling?

We liked each other all this time, secretly pined, and we've missed out on being together because I've been too afraid to rock the boat or upset my parents. I didn't want to hurt Hector, but I'm ultimately hurting him more by playing pretend.

I've been so wrong.

As scared as I am, when we get out of this, I have to make it right.

I want Jake. He's my missing piece, but it's up to me to make that a reality.

I—

"It's not right."

A harsh voice jolts me. My eyes snap open, the morning haze turning to crystal clarity as I hear the gravelly complaint.

"JT's batshit crazy, man," a new voice chimes in.

Jake shifts behind me, moving in slow motion so as not to make any noise.

"He's always been obsessed with that woman. You shouldn't have told him where Alejandro would be this weekend."

"I know that now. I just heard about it and passed it on. I thought I was doing him a favor. The guy's been miserable since she ran away. She just cut out, and

Alejandro helped her do it. That was unfair, you know? She shouldn't have done it like that."

"She was probably just scared."

Jake's jacket rustles as he slowly rises to his feet. We both wince and go perfectly still, staring at each other with wide eyes and trying not to breathe.

The voices are coming closer.

"I never thought JT would take it this far. He said we were going *hunting*. He never said our prey was human."

They fall silent for a moment. I lick my lips, the cold air turning the moisture icy. We have to get up and start running. Or is it better to lie low and let them pass us?

But they're coming this way!

They'll probably stumble across us if we don't move.

"We should just bail, man. Radio in that we're done and be gone."

"We can't do that!" the gruff voice thunders.

Jake takes advantage of the noise and moves to his feet. He probably wants to run and grab his pack, but we might just have to do without it. I reach for his wrist, freezing when the voices draw another foot closer.

"Axel, look at me. We're in this 'til the end. You want to go to jail? If they escape this place and show anyone that footage, that's what's gonna happen. We'll be implicated. Even if we didn't stab him, we stood there watching, and that makes us guilty. The only way out of this is to get rid of all the evidence. *All* of it."

My nostrils flare, fear spiking through me as I get to my feet, ready to run.

Jake's body is angled toward the tree where his pack is

hiding.

"Do you think we should—" My whisper is cut off when the branches to our right suddenly snap. I spin to check out the noise and come face-to-face with the barrel of a hunting rifle.

I gasp, my entire body turning to rigid stone.

"I've got you now." The man's dark eyes gleam as he shouts, "I've got 'em! Over here!"

I want to turn and see what Jake's doing, but I'm frozen, my gaze locked on the gun facing me. I've always hated guns. Having one aimed at me is only reaffirming my anti-gun stance.

Heavy feet crash through the brush as the air in my lungs grows thin.

Seconds later, two men charge into the little clearing, relief washing over their faces. One of them snatches my arm, pulling me off my feet.

I yelp and start to fall, but he hauls me up again.

"Let her go," Jake snarls, lashing out with his fist to bash the guy next to him.

It doesn't work, and he's grabbed by the collar and thrown back against a tree. He groans and lands with a sad thud on the ground. The gun that was aimed at me drops away. The guy slings it over his back, crouching down to search Jake's pockets.

Jake slaps his hands away, his eyes flaring with anger when the man reaches for him and tries again.

"Get off me," he spits, trying to shove the man away.

It scores him a slap to the face.

"Where is it?" the man barks. "Where!"

Jake remains silent. The angry red mark on his face must sting, but he presses his lips into a stubborn, thin line.

The guy grunts, then turns his menacing glare onto me.

I flinch and look to the ground.

"Where!" he shouts, standing to his feet and storming toward me.

I recognize him with his big mustache and muscly build. He's not the one who killed Alejandro, but he was standing right there, his gun aimed at my friend.

I cower against the guy who's holding my arm. His fingers are digging in, and it kind of hurts, but—

"They're just kids, man." The man with green eyes runs a hand over his bald head, looking apprehensive about this whole thing.

He could end up being an ally. I throw him a desperate look, but he glances away from me when Mr. Mustache starts yelling.

"I don't give a shit how old they are. They've got something I want, and we're not leaving here without it!" He spins toward Jake, fisting his jacket and pulling him to his feet. "Give us the card."

A muscle in Jake's jaw clenches, but he stares the guy down, perfectly calm as he softly says, "I don't know what you're talking about."

The man snarls in disgust, letting Jake go, then rocketing a fist at his face. The connection is a brutal one. Jake buckles like he's been hit with a battering ram.

I scream when he drops to the dirt with a soft groan.

"Shut up!" The guy points at me, his bushy eyebrows dipping into an intimidating V.

Jake lets out a small grunt, touching his tender face and wiping blood from his lip. That must have hurt so bad, but he's trying not to let it show.

The scary man grabs his arm, hauling him back to his feet and spitting in his face, "You know exactly what I'm talking about. The card! The one that was missing from the camera you left behind! We know you've got it. Now cough it up, and we might just let you live."

"I don't have it," Jake murmurs.

The lie scores him a punch to the stomach. He doubles over, gasping for air. Saliva pools on his lip, and he drops to his knees. His mouth opens like he's fighting for oxygen that doesn't exist.

The man uses his boot to shove Jake off balance. He flops onto the forest floor and scores a kick to the torso, then another punch to the face. The guy's full force crashes into Jake, leaving him dazed and bloody.

"No! Stop!" I scream. *"¡Desgraciados! ¡Déjenlo ir! ¡Déjennos en paz! ¡No vuelvas a ponerle una mano encima! ¡Te odio por hacerle daño! ¡Déjenme ir! ¡Déjennos ir!"*

"Would you shut her up?" Mr. Mustache points at the guy holding me, and suddenly a sweaty, dirt-stained hand clamps over my mouth, cutting off my curses, insults, and futile threats.

I scream and writhe to get him off me. His hand smells disgusting, and I grab his arm, trying to pull him away, but he just pinches tighter. My teeth cut into my cheek, and I feel like he's going to break my jaw.

"Let her go!" Jake croaks from the ground. "Please! Let her go!"

"Not until you give me that card."

Jake's eyes shoot to mine, and we hold a silent conversation. He wants to give it up for my sake, but he can't do that.

I try to shake my head, but I'm stuck. The guy has me pinned against him, his beefy arm squeezing my waist, his sweaty hand across my lips.

The other guy, the one who noticed how young we are, has his gun half-heartedly trained on Jake while Mr. Punch looks ready to dish out some more torture. I don't want Jake to get hurt, but should we be giving up our only bargaining chip?

I don't know how to play this.

My eyes smart as I stare at Jake. He's wrestling with the same questions I am.

What should we do?

"Not gonna talk? That's fine. Let's see if your girl has something to say." He whips a knife off his belt and steps toward me.

"Kane! What are you doing?"

"Shut up, Axel. This has to be done."

Pressing the knife to my throat, he gives me a leering smirk. "Take your hand off her mouth, Jonesy. Let's see if we can get her talking."

"No!" Jake goes to stand but is shoved back down by a boot to his shoulder. He lands with a grunt, and I see the pain wash over his face.

"You know where that card is?" Kane runs the knife

blade up my neck, the sharp metal teasing my skin as it glides around my chin and lightly over my trembling mouth.

He's gonna cut me.

It's gonna hurt.

Tears blind me, the thinning air in my lungs making me light-headed.

I need Ademir. But he's dead. I'm gonna be dead too.

My chest starts heaving, a pitiful whimper escaping as I try to lean away from the knife but can't.

"I hid it!" Jake shouts, blood spitting out of his mouth. "It's not with me."

The blade stops against my bottom lip, a light warning pressure that reminds me to stay still. Kane whips around to bark at Jake.

"Where is it, then?"

Jake spits again, licking his glossy red lips and trying to sit up. Axel relents, and I feel Jake's pain as he shifts position, his beaten body obviously hurting all over. "As soon as I tell you, you're gonna kill us." He swallows and has the guts to glare at Kane. "I'm not telling you shit until you let her go and guarantee she'll get out of this alive."

He's bargaining for me.

He's trying to save my life. That's so Jake.

He'd sacrifice himself for me, I know he would.

I can't let that happen. We're either walking out of here together or not at all.

Think, Carmen! Think!

31

STAYING ALIVE

Jake

KANE SMIRKS DOWN AT ME. I glare at him, silently demanding he take that knife away from Carmen's mouth. His jaw works to the side, making me wait it out for a moment before stepping away.

The color has drained from Carmen's face, but her lips are red, a small bead of blood forming where he pressed the blade too hard.

I want to rip his frickin' head off for hurting her. I wish I could.

I wish Brody was here. He'd bust heads. So would Deeks. He was always the feisty one. Cooper would quietly stand over me like a guardian angel while Michael showed me the fastest escape route, the best place to hide.

That ache in my chest grows again—that yearning for something I no longer have.

It's just me right now, so I let my eyes do the talking, telling that asshole exactly how I feel. He saunters over to me with a snicker, making me small and pitiful.

Before he can grab my shirt and haul me up, I stand, facing him head-on. Pain ricochets through my body. My stomach is killing me and my face is still throbbing, but I'm not letting any of that show. I have to stay calm. I can't beat this guy with physical strength, but maybe I can outsmart him.

My eyes dart to Carmen. She's looking at the ground, her skin almost white, her bottom lip trembling. She hasn't bothered to wipe the blood away, and one lone drop is making its way to her chin. I move toward her, but Kane blocks my way, pulling the radio off his belt.

"Come in, JT." The radio blips and crackles as we wait for a response.

"Yeah."

"We've got what you were looking for."

"No shit." He starts to laugh. "Did you get what we need?"

"Kid says he doesn't have it."

I try to catch Carmen's eye. The big guy is holding her arm too tight. I can see his fingers digging in. He's hurting her!

"Well, where the hell is it?" JT's voice is interrupted by a little static.

Kane presses the button again. "He says he's hidden it somewhere but won't tell us unless we guarantee the girl's safety."

"Aw, bullshit! Bring him to me. I'll get him talking."

A cold chill sweeps through me, the words ominous and terror-inducing.

Can I handle torture?

I'm in enough pain as it is.

Am I strong enough to withstand more than what's already been inflicted?

I don't want to break. Alejandro deserves justice. We have to protect Donita. I—

"Start heading southeast. We'll meet you in a few minutes."

"Got it. Over and out." Kane glances among his hunting buddies, his bushy mustache twitching when his lips curl into a crooked grin. Pointing his radio in the right direction, he barks, "Let's go!"

A gun nudges my back, and I'm shunted forward.

Carmen's eyes bulge with fear. I have to get her out of this, but I'm one guy. I can't fight off three larger men with guns. I'll be dead after one move.

My brain starts scrambling for an out. Words have always been my best form of defense. I'll just have to talk my way out of this, lie until JT believes me.

Shit, this is bad.

My feet stumble across the terrain as we're pushed and nudged forward. My bag and all its contents are still tucked high in that tree. I'm a little lost without it, like I'm no use if I can't whip something from my pack and problem-solve the moment. How can I protect Carmen without my stuff?

She's shunted to the left and ends up beside me. She doesn't respond to the rough treatment, and I'm worried about her. Her breaths are too punchy, like she's about to have a panic attack. Her skin's so pale, her eyes so huge, darting around the forest like lost prey. But she won't look at me. She blinks rapidly.

Is she fighting tears?

I'm about to open my mouth and tell her to breathe and stay calm when she jolts to a stop and throws her head backward.

I jerk with surprise as the guy behind me howls and clutches his nose. Carmen whips around, slashing out with her hand and doing some kind of karate chop maneuver to his throat. He chokes and crumples to his knees, gasping for air.

"What the f—" Kane whips around to see what's going on, but before he can finish his sentence, Carmen's grabbed my wrist and we're plowing through the forest, slapping at branches and shrubs as we sprint for our lives.

"Shoot them!" a shout echoes behind us.

"They're just kids!"

"Argh, you idiot!"

I pick up my pace, vaulting over tree roots and surging ahead. My body is raging at me—each jolt and misstep fires a new agony to a different part of me, but I can't stop.

Move, man. Move!

A gunshot booms, and we both duck as the tree beside

us explodes, firing splinters into the air. Carmen yelps but keeps on running, and I cover her back, following her to who knows where.

"You missed?" Kane roars. "Some fucking hunter you are! Go and find them! How could you just let them go! And you, get up! Get! UP!"

"Keep going," I puff, pushing Carmen's back when her pace starts to slow. "We gotta move."

Carmen pumps her arms and picks up speed. I follow closely, praying we can make it. Praying we'll stumble across some kind of out.

We're trying to outrun hunters—guys who track prey for a hobby. Men with guns who could take us out long-range and we might not even see it coming.

The odds are stacked so high against us, it's a joke.

But still I keep moving.

Because I have to try.

I can't leave this world without doing everything in my power to stay in it.

32

A PLEA FOR HELP

Carmen

MY LEGS ARE GOING to give out any second now.

I've never run this fast for this long before. My lungs are burning, I'm puffing like a rhino, but I have to keep moving forward. My life literally depends on it.

Ignoring the pain in my muscles, I push ahead, glancing over my shoulder to make sure Jake's still behind me.

His face is scrunched with a grimace, and I wonder how much he's still hurting from that brutal beating. It looked so painful.

"I'm okay. Keep going!" He points ahead of us, and I do as he says, slapping more branches away as we plow through the uncharted forest. The ground is undulating and unforgiving, my knees and ankles paying a price with each misstep. I have no idea where this route is leading us. It could be to the edge of a freaking cliff.

All I know is guns are coming and that's a definite. So we go forward.

Turning sideways, I bust through a thick crop of trees and stumble out into a small clearing.

"No way," I whisper, blinking twice to make sure I'm not hallucinating.

"Yes," Jake breathes beside me, placing his hand on my back and pushing me toward the rundown cabin we've just discovered.

It's small and dark with a cracked window by the door. It's obvious no one has lived here in a long time, but it's still a place to hide.

I turn the rusted handle, but the door won't budge.

"Lean into it." Jake thumps his shoulder against the solid wood.

I join him, and after a hard shove, the door pops open and we fly through it, landing in a heap on the dirty floor.

Yeah, we're going to be black and blue by the end of this.

I groan and try to sit up.

Jake scrambles off me, helping me stand and gazing around the unkempt cabin. Spiders and insects have turned this deserted place into a mansion, cobwebs decorating every corner of the room.

There's a dusty old mattress beneath the back window

and a small kitchen with canned goods still stacked on the open shelves.

Jake rushes past me, bumping his hip on the table as he yanks open cupboards and drawers. "There must be something we can use around here. An old radio? Something!"

I crouch down, checking the drawers near the mattress. Yanking the top one open, I rifle through the contents and spot a map near the bottom.

Please, please, please!

"Yes! A map." I rush over to the table, unfolding it and spreading my hands across the paper to flatten it. "Is this where we are?" I punch my finger into the dense section of green. There's a highlighted route leading from a ranger station to this spot. "That's gotta be it, right?"

"Is this the river we crossed?" Jake scans the map, pointing at the squiggly blue line, but there are so many squiggly blue lines, and there's more than one ranger station too!

"We came in at Ely."

We both lean over the map, frantically searching for place names and trying to work out if this highlighted route is something we can trust.

"We have to assume it is."

"I think that's the station we left from." I tap my finger on it, noticing how dirty my nails are.

Gross. Curling them into a fist, I keep scanning the map, trying to figure out which trails we hiked while filming and where we might be. I can picture the beautiful spots, but trying to transfer that onto a map is so difficult, especially when panic is pulsing just below the surface, threatening to take me out at any moment.

My insides are going nuts, my mind starting to scatter as the growing threat gets nearer. We're no longer moving, and they could catch up to us at any moment. Can we seriously hide in this cabin? Where? We're suddenly sitting ducks.

"We need to move." I shake my head, itching to snatch the map and run. "We're just gonna have to trust that highlighted route and assume the X is this cabin." I tap my nail on it, an erratic staccato.

"We need to find a radio or something. We have to call for help."

I spin away from Jake, throwing open any cupboard I can. Desperation builds as I hit another empty shelf.

"Let me work out the coordinates," Jake mutters under his breath, and I want to scream at him that it's no use if those hunters catch up to us.

We need to go! Now!

Ripping open the last cupboard in the kitchen, I stop short when I notice a black box. I yank it out, flipping back the lid.

"A… a sat phone!" I sputter, rushing back to the table and slapping it down. "Is this a satellite phone?"

Jake gapes at it for a moment, then snatches it out of the case. "Please, God, let it be working."

He starts punching in numbers.

"Who are you calling?"

"My brother."

"Shouldn't we be calling the police?"

He glances at me, like it hadn't occurred to him, but then he jolts, his eyes growing wide. "Brody!... We're in trouble. We need help. These guys are chasing us. They want to kill us. I've got something on them that's a big deal. I swear, man, this is huge!... You have to get help!"

Jake winces like he's straining to hear what his brother's saying. Then his eyes round and he spins to face the map again. "Superior National Forest. Boundary Waters! We've found this little hunting cabin, and I think the coordinates are..." He rattles them off and I bite my lip, glancing to the cracked window, thinking I hear shouts outside. "I need you to alert the authorities. We have information they have to see."

I think I hear thundering feet and snatch Jake's jacket, giving it a good shake. "They're coming. We gotta go!"

"These killers are after us. We—"

A bullet smashes through the kitchen window. I scream and drop to my knees, tugging on Jake's pant leg. "Get down!"

He drops beside me, covering my head with his arms when another spray of bullets takes out the window by the door.

"We gotta move." Snatching my arm, he pulls me across the room. We scramble over the wooden floor, crawling to the mattress and the window just above it.

All the gunfire is focused at the front of the cabin right now. If we're lucky, they'll be so intent on riddling the cabin with bullets that we can sneak away undetected.

"Come on." Jake shoves the window open, then pulls me forward and practically throws me through it.

I land on my hands, then roll across the dirt, getting to my feet as Jake flops out of the gap and clambers up to a run.

I move in beside him, pumping my arms and sprinting yet again. I don't know how much longer we can do this. Brody better act fast.

I can't believe Jake called his brother instead of the police. What was he thinking?

Repeated gunfire makes me duck my head. I swallow the scream rising up my throat as fear tries to take me out at the knees.

Keep running, Carmen. Don't you stop.

Help is on the way. I have to hold on to that truth.

Help is coming.

But will it come in time?

33

BULLET HOLES IN THE BOATSHED

Jake

MY BODY IS SCREAMING—BEGGING me to stop, collapse, lie down and never move again. But I don't have that luxury. Pain vibrates from my center, clawing down each limb and warning me that I may not have a choice.

We have to find shelter. A place to hide until the cavalry arrives. I know it will. Brody would do anything for me. Indy is no doubt nearby. She's the daughter of a man with influence. If anyone can make something happen in a hurry, it'll be her.

We just have to last.

But I can't keep up this pace, and those bullets are gonna reach us any second.

We careen down the hill, my body protesting with spikes of pain driving through me each step of the way. My knee buckles and I nearly fall but manage to stumble and right myself in time. Carmen spins back to check on me, her eyes bulging in surprise before she rushes back and takes my hand, pulling me along.

She's showing grit and determination. The fierce look in her brown eyes is making my heart stutter. If I didn't love her before... I shake my head in wonder at this new layer she's revealed.

She's everything.

We have to survive this so we can be together. Legit together. No more pining from the sidelines. I want to claim this woman, walk down the street holding her hand, call her my girlfriend, kiss her before falling asleep, wrap my arms around her beautiful body. I want—

Another gunshot makes me flinch. I skid on a clump of pine needles and crash to the ground, nearly bringing Carmen with me. She yelps, but I release her in time and she doesn't drop. Pain fires through my hip and elbow. I hiss and force my aching body back up.

"You can do it," Carmen whispers. "Come on! Come on! We gotta run."

I take her hand again, and we dodge trees like we're running the final play of a football game. Everything is on the line. All we have to do is reach the end zone!

"What's that ahead?" Carmen picks up her pace, pulling us down to the edge of a lake. There's a big clearing which makes me feel totally exposed. We're sitting ducks out here.

"There!" Carmen points farther down the slope to our right, and I spot the top of a rusty iron roof. "Let's go."

She releases my hand so we can sprint the final part side by side. Scrambling down the hill, we slip and slide until we reach an old-looking boatshed. The door is bolted shut with a chain, but it's loose enough that we can pull the door wide and squeeze through the narrow gap.

I'm not sure if securing ourselves in here is the best idea. We're cutting off an escape route, but the idea of hiding in a dark corner and waiting it out is pretty damn appealing. If they didn't see us run this way, then we might be in the clear.

My body needs to stop. My heart is racing so fast it's like a ticking bomb, and my lungs are burning. Every ache and pain is throbbing through me, so when Carmen pulls me past the rows of canoes, then drops to her knees and starts crawling into a dark space behind them, I follow her without question.

She sits on her butt, pulling her knees to her chin and turning herself into a ball. I wriggle in next to her. It hurts, but I lift my arm over her shoulders and nestle her against me. Her thick hair tickles my face, and I tuck it under my chin, gripping her shoulder until she's so close we could be one person.

Her breathing is quick and erratic. I wonder if stopping is causing the panic to catch up with her.

I kiss her head and whisper, "It's okay. We're gonna make it." We both know that's highly unlikely, but I say it anyway. "Donita needs us to make it."

Carmen curls her fingers into my jacket, pressing her

head against my shoulder. "If... I mean *when* we survive this... when it's all over... what are you gonna do?"

"Kiss you," I rasp. "As much as I can."

She lets out a soft snicker, then sniffs like she's fighting tears. I wish I could see her face, but it's not like there's much room to move in here.

"I'm gonna make things right with my parents. Tell Hector it's absolutely over. Fight for what makes me happy."

My heart starts to shine. I can feel the rays bursting through my chest and for a brief moment worry that the bright beams will give away our location.

Yeah, there's a chance I have a concussion.

"You need to forgive your brothers." Carmen's words snap me back to reality. "You need to go see them. If... *when* we get out of this, promise me you'll at least hear what they have to say."

I can't speak, emotion clogging my throat. Someone's shoving balls of cotton down my airways, I swear.

"Jake, you have to promise." Carmen shakes my jacket. "I'd do anything to see my brother again. They want you back in their lives. You can't cut them out. Please." Her voice trembles, and I know she's crying.

It takes me a moment to inhale. I can't give her a flippant "Okay" just to ease the tears. I have to be honest.

"Please say you will."

"I will," I finally croak.

She sags with relief against me, then carefully wriggles around so she can look up at me. I think she wants to say something but somehow can't. Her eyes are drinking me in, the dim light not diminishing the emotion I can see. I'm important to her. I matter so freaking much.

I love you. The words are right there, on the tip of my tongue.

Do I tell her?

Is it too soon?

You could be dead in a minute. Say it! Say it!

"Carmen." I whisper her name like it's the sweetest sound in the world, because it is. Brushing the pads of my fingers down her tear-streaked face, I let the feels pulse through me. Overwhelming waves of... of love. Pressing my lips against hers, I taste the salty tears and relish her soft whimper, the way she squeezes the back of my neck, the desperation of her lips as they crush against mine.

Please, God, don't let this be our last kiss.

Pounding feet draw closer, the danger rearing over us. A sick reminder.

Rhinos are coming, their deadly horns ready to split us in half.

We pull away from each other, but our eyes stay locked in place.

"Carmen, I—"

"There! The shed!"

"Just shoot the shit out of it! If they're in there, we'll end them."

"What about the SD card?"

"Just shoot it!"

Bullets start hitting the boatshed.

Carmen's screams are muffled by the explosive noise. She ducks her head and I cover her with my arms, tucking my body around her to try and shield her face from the flying splinters of wood. Canoes start to clatter on their shelves, rattling and falling.

We're in the middle of chaos.

They're going to pepper this structure with bullets and holes until it falls down around us. My insides thrum with that knowledge, and for some reason, all I can see are my brothers. Deeks, Michael, standing outside my dorm, desperate for me to hear them out.

I'm not gonna get that chance anymore. Sadness sweeps through me, a new kind I haven't felt before. It's soul-crushing, that realization that I pushed them out of my life. My brothers. My family.

Grandpa, I'm sorry.

He'd be so disappointed. He did everything in his power to rescue us, teach us, keep us together. He'd be heartsick over my behavior.

I'll make it right. Get us out of this and I'll make it right, I swear.

And like some miracle from heaven, the gunfire is disrupted by a sound.

Whip-whip-whip.

It's rhythmic. It's—

My head pops up, my ears straining to hear what I think are chopper blades.

"Is that...?" I whisper, straining some more until I know for sure that a helicopter is hovering nearby. "The cavalry."

"What?" Carmen glances up, her eyes large and bright.

"Do you hear that?"

The gunfire falters as the whipping blades draw closer.

"Helicopter," Carmen whispers like she's afraid to believe it. "Is that for us?"

"It better be." I let out a sigh of relief, especially when I hear the panic outside.

"Shit! Run! Move, move, move!"

"I told you we took things too far!"

"JT, you asshole!"

"Shut the hell up and run!"

I close my eyes, leaning my head back and whispering, "Thank you, Brody."

This wired, high-pitched, weird sound pops out of me. It's probably an attempt at laughter, but I'm not really sure.

"This is the police. Lower your weapons and put your hands up!"

We wait out the yelling and scuffling. I'm guessing there's some kind of chase going on, but I can't be sure. No bullets are flying, so that's a good sign, right?

Easing away from Carmen, I start to crawl out of our hiding spot.

"What are you doing?" She snatches my jacket.

"I think it's safe now."

"You sure?" Her eyes are wide and beautiful.

I stop to smile at her, running my fingers down her dirty face. "Yes. I'm sure."

Cautiously making our way to the boatshed doors, we listen by the entrance for a moment, then finally find the courage to reveal ourselves.

34

PLEASE HELP ME, GOD

Carmen

I'M STILL nervous to go outside, but Jake takes my hand and pulls us through the gap between the doors. The poor boatshed is pretty beat up, holes covering the doors and walls.

Bullet holes.

Bullets that could have ripped through our flesh and killed us.

I lean against the wood, suddenly overwhelmed by that thought.

We could have died. So easily.

My parents. They'd be beside themselves. They barely

coped with the loss of their son, but to lose their daughter too?

"It's okay." Jake squeezes my hand. "It's safe."

We creep into the opening, checking out what's happening before revealing ourselves.

A park ranger and three police officers have surrounded the men. They're lying on the packed dirt, hands zip-tied behind their backs. All five of them. Thank God.

I look away, not wanting to stare at them. As triumphant as their capture is, it's a sick victory. This shouldn't have happened. Alejandro should be here with us. It's not right!

"Find the kids!" someone is shouting.

"Here!" Jake steps into the open, raising his hand.

The authorities rush toward us. "Hands up!"

"What?" My eyes bulge, my hands automatically rising as I throw a panicked look at Jake.

He gives me a calm smile and awkwardly drops to his knees when the officer tells him to. "My name is Jake Adams. You would have received a call from my twin brother, Brody, or his girlfriend, Indigo Shaw... or maybe her father, Castle Shaw? We entered this area a few days ago, logged our route at the ranger station near Ely. Alejandro Gomez was our guide." Jake's voice quavers, and my eyes start to burn, tears blurring my vision.

Alejandro. Such a good man. Now gone.

The loss settles on my shoulders like a weight I can't bear. I slump forward, suddenly exhausted, my soul crushed to ash. At least his killers will be brought to justice now, but how will that help Donita? She's still lost the man she loved. The one who saved her from JT.

I close my eyes, letting the tears slowly trickle down my cheeks as the police move around us, patting us down for any weapons, before finally letting us rise. I help Jake stand, wrapping my arm around his waist to support him.

"Radio it in!" A man with salt-and-pepper whiskers runs toward us, his eyes awash with worry as he checks out Jake's beat-up face and then glances at me. "You guys all right?"

"We are now." Jake wraps his arm around my shoulders, squeezing me close.

"I'm Ranger Mitch Hamilton. Let's get you guys out of here."

We're led toward a second chopper, which must have arrived with the first. I turned the noise into one, but the cavalry definitely arrived with flair.

"How'd you know where we were?" I shout above the din of the blades, ducking my head and entering the helicopter the way I'm shown how.

The man waits until I'm seated before turning to me with a friendly smile.

"About a day and a half ago, two scared guys turned up at the ranger station, ranting about hunters with guns. It took us a while to figure out what they were trying to tell us."

The chopper lifts into the air and I jolt, snatching Jake's arm. He rubs his hand gently over mine and gives me a reassuring smile.

"So we've been looking for you," the man continues.

"And then we get a phone call with your exact coordinates. Well, nearly exact." His smile is broad with wonder as he shakes his head. "Man, did we show up on time. Glad we had the police with us. Those guys were dead set on ending you two."

"Don't we know it," Jake shouts, then wrestles in his pocket for the card. He struggles to pull it free, so I help him and then hold out the card in my open palm.

"This has everything you need. Proof of exactly what happened."

The man's expression sobers up. "So, it is true. Murder, huh?"

We nod in unison, the weight of that statement heavy with sorrow.

"It's a tragic loss," the ranger murmurs. "Alejandro was a good man. I didn't know him personally, but the other rangers always spoke really highly of him."

The words burn like a hot poker. *Why do the good get taken?* Blinking at even more tears, I turn away from the man, watching the sky flash by as we head for safety.

"I'm just glad you managed to get away. You two are amazing, truly." The ranger shakes his head in obvious awe.

Jake grins and looks at me. "Well, this girl's got some mean moves. She saved our lives."

I gape at him and shake my head. "No way. I couldn't have survived this without you."

"Sounds like you two make a good team!"

I turn away from the ranger's wink and focus on Jake.

He leans his forehead against mine and whispers, "We do."

I press my lips together and let my dimples do the talking for me.

"Where did you learn to kick ass like that, by the way?"

I swallow. "My brother taught me."

Jake squeezes my hand, understanding the importance of that simple statement.

"I guess desperation reminded me what to do."

"I'm glad it did." Jake rests his head back, closing his eyes and looking slightly sick. I wonder if the helicopter ride is upsetting his stomach. I can understand why; the poor guy got beat pretty bad. His whole system is probably wrestling to function properly.

I gaze out the window, the shock of everything catching up to me. A dull headache is thumping behind my eyes as the adrenaline starts to fade.

The last few days have been harrowing, emotional, overwhelming.

But it's over now.

We're safe, and we have all the evidence we need to put those five men away. Donita can grieve without the threat of JT hanging over her. Hopefully she can move on with her life, knowing he's locked away and he can't hurt her again.

Justice will be served.

So, we can rest.

I lean my head against Jake's shoulder and close my eyes as an unsettling realization washes over me.

No. Wait.

I can't rest.

Not yet.

There are still things to be said—to Hector, to my parents.

Bile swirls in my belly.

Jake rests his cheek against the top of my head, and I focus on that feeling—the rightness of it all.

We make a good team.

We do.

Jake and Carmen, that's what I want.

And so I have to face this bile, this dread, because if I don't, I'll stay trapped in a life that's slowly ending me. A half-life where I pretend I'm happy, but deep down I'm just left unsatisfied.

A life with Jake wouldn't be that way.

I have to fight for it.

I just pray I have the strength and courage.

Por favor, Dios, ayúdame.

35

A NOTEPAD AND A CUP OF COFFEE

Jake

THE TRIP to the ranger's station is quick. As soon as the helicopter lands, we're ushered into the log cabin-style structure where a couple paramedics are waiting to check us out.

Carmen's hand is still in mine, but the second we walk through the door, Hector comes rushing toward us. Pulling Carmen away from me, he wraps his arms around her, kissing her face and saying over and over again, "Thank God you're all right." Holding her face, he studies her with glassy eyes. "Are you hurt?"

"I'm fine," she whispers.

"Your lip's cut."

"I'm fine."

"This way please, sir." Someone has my elbow and is guiding me to sit down. The paramedic then starts asking me about my injuries. I reply in a monotone, my gaze locked on Hector and Carmen. He's holding her again, his arms engulfing her so I can't even see her face anymore.

She hugs him back, her dirty jacket sleeves wrapping around his waist, and I'm massacred with doubts.

Did everything we experienced over the weekend mean nothing?

Those two nights we slept side by side suddenly turn to vapor as reality kicks back in. Like a freaking steel-capped boot to the butt.

Hector still thinks he and Carmen are together. Will she have the strength to let him down? Will she have the courage to tell her parents what she really wants?

And what about me?

Will I have the courage to face my brothers the way I promised?

"Ouch." I flinch when the paramedic starts poking at my ribs.

Carmen breaks away from Hector, studying me with a worried frown. I look to the floor, clenching me teeth.

"You've got some nasty bruising on your torso." Gloved fingers gently inspect my wounds.

"That tends to happen when you're kicked repeatedly."

"You could have some fractures here. We need to get you x-rayed at the hospital."

I close my eyes, wishing I could deny them and demand to get on a flight home. I want my dorm room.

Someplace quiet where I can hide away and lick my wounds.

The adrenaline is starting to evaporate from my body, replaced with an exhausting weight that wants to drag me right through the floor.

"We'll need a statement. You think you're up for that before we transport you to the hospital?" someone says.

I open my eyes and notice an officer hovering over me.

My shoulder hitches.

Carmen takes a seat on one of the chairs opposite me while the police officer pulls out a notepad and looks between us.

It takes me back in time for a second. I stare at the notebook, suddenly seeing the sheriff. At least I can tell the truth this time. There's nothing to hide.

Hector wraps his fingers around Carmen's hand. Her grip is loose, but she's not pulling away. I stare at their connection, my mind buzzing with disappointment. I can feel myself shifting into robotic mode—no emotion, no pain.

"So, can you run me through the events of what happened?" Leaning his elbows on his knees, the officer gives me a kind smile before turning to Carmen.

Neither of us can say anything, and I know I need to step up and talk, just to get this over with.

But then Carmen sniffs, her voice wavering as she rasps, "They killed Alejandro. Murdered him."

Hector puts his arm around her shoulders, pulling her close and kissing the side of her head. She closes her eyes, tears trickling down her cheeks when she leans into his embrace.

I swallow the acidic ash in my throat and dig the memory card out of my pocket again.

"I got the whole thing on camera." I slap the small plastic square into the police officer's palm. "It should all be there."

"This is amazing," the officer murmurs, placing it into an evidence bag.

"We tried to tell them what we could," Hector mumbles, running a hand through his hair, "but we didn't know much. We thought you guys were behind us, but then we realized it was hunters and we hid for hours until we were sure the coast was clear. Then we followed the trail to the ranger's station."

"We've been looking for you ever since," Lenny pipes up. I only just notice he's here. He's dirty and pale, like he hasn't slept in days. I get that feeling.

Swiping a hand under my nose, I nod, not sure what to say. Shock must be catching up to me or something because I'm feeling kind of fuzzy and sick. I hold my head in my hands, my weak arms like matchsticks as I rest them on my knees and try to stay upright.

"We can do this at the hospital, if you like." The officer's soft voice reaches me, and I immediately shake my head.

"No. I want to get this done. We need to go home."

I glance up and share a brief look with Carmen. Her large eyes are drinking me in, but I don't know what she's thinking. I glance at her lips, remembering their soft, supple beauty for a fleeting moment. Will I ever feel them on me again?

She dips her head, letting Hector pull her against his chest.

My heart deflates, withering inside like a dried-up raisin.

Just get this done, man. Get it done and get out!

Clearing my throat, I sit up and force myself to focus. With robotic efficiency, I run through the events of the weekend, leaving out any parts about me and Carmen together and focusing solely on what we saw and how we tried to get back.

"We didn't think to search past the river. We figured you were trying to head back here." The ranger hands me a steaming mug of coffee.

I sip at it, grateful for the caffeine kick.

"We didn't know which direction it was." Carmen wraps her elegant fingers around her mug. "Alejandro figured out all the details with you, and when we first ran from the campsite, our number one goal was not to get shot. By the time we stopped running, we had no idea where we were."

"We figured south was our best bet, but that's all we had, really. And then we fell in the river and..." I spun my hand in the air, hoping that would suffice for words. I've already said all this stuff and don't want to go through it yet again.

"Well, that phone call we got from your brother was key." Ranger Hamilton nodded, his smile warm with admiration. "You did the right thing calling him. Good job."

"We're just lucky we found that phone."

My soft statement is followed by a heavy silence, and I guarantee we're all thinking the same thing—if we hadn't, we'd be dead.

Compelled by a force I can't counter, my gaze travels to Carmen. She stares back, and all I can lament is how damn beautiful she is and how badly I want her to be mine.

36

UGLY WORDS AND FLUTTERING HEARTBEATS

Carmen

EVERYTHING TAKES FOREVER—THE interview, the drive to the hospital, waiting for X-rays. Hector tries to get me to leave, but I refuse to go anywhere until Jake has been cleared.

Turns out his ribs are perfectly intact, but he has some major bruising, and he needs to take it easy for a few days. It took everything in me not to wrap Jake in a crushing hug, I was so relieved, but Hector was hovering right beside me, and Lenny was standing there too.

I feel like I can't breathe.

It's nearing dusk when we finally board a private jet —arranged by Castle Shaw—to fly back to the West

Coast. Jake's been on the phone with his brother every spare moment, and I haven't had a chance to talk to him. It doesn't help that Hector won't let go of my hand. It's like he's afraid to let me out of his sight or something.

Is he remembering our fight? What I said to him?

Or is he just choosing to ignore it?

I have to say something to him.

Glancing at his tired face, I wonder if this small plane with everyone sitting so close is the right place to do it.

Talk about awkward.

No, I'll wait until we get back.

"You okay?" Hector rubs the back of my hand with his thumb.

I nod, staring at our connection before looking for Jake. He's resting in the plush chair adjacent to me with his eyes closed, but he looks too tense to be asleep. Maybe he's just faking it so he doesn't have to watch Hector and me together like a couple.

Flashes of the past few days scream through me—the fear, the adrenaline, the kissing. The warm memory of sleeping in Jake's arms wraps around me like a fluffy comforter. We worked so well together, made the perfect team as we fought to stay alive and get out of there.

And now I'm right back where I started. With Hector. Afraid to speak my mind.

I can't do that again.

I have to face the thing I've been fearing the most —honesty.

It's weird how I've just survived death, yet the idea of

unwrapping my feelings and telling the truth is terrifying me.

I nibble the inside of my cheek, trying to formulate a breakup speech as we head back home. By the time we land, I'm truly exhausted and not sure I'm capable of speech at all.

We disembark onto the runway and are met by a group of people all desperate to see us. They come running forward with arms flung wide. I spot Brody next to a girl who must be Indigo Shaw. Hector's mother is already crying when she reaches him, rising to her tiptoes to wrap her son in a hug.

"Carmen, *mi bebé*." Mamá rushes forward, capturing me against her and starting to sob.

"*Hola, Mamá*." I hold her tight and am soon wrapped in Papá's embrace too. He engulfs us both, kissing my head and murmuring endearments under his breath.

"*Gracias a Dios que estás a salvo.*"

Thank God I'm safe. He says it over and over until it's a lullaby in my ear.

I rest against my parents for I don't know how long as we cry together, releasing the fear of near death and then mourning the loss of sweet Alejandro. Mamá blubbers in Spanish, remembering what a kind child he was, which then leads her to talk about Ademir too.

They were best friends. So alike. How could this happen? Why do the brave, the wonderful, get taken? It's not fair. It's not fair.

Papá calms her in a soothing voice, and I'm hugged a little tighter.

"Carmen is alive, Antonella. Hold your daughter. She is safe. We still have her."

Mamá kisses my chin, my cheeks, my tears, and thanks God repeatedly that I made it out alive.

Eventually the tang of aviation fuel and the cool night air pulls us apart. Papá rests his hand on my lower back, guiding me to the car. I strain away from him, wanting to see Jake and make sure he's okay. Now that Hector and my parents aren't attached to me, I feel like I can move again.

"Papá, I need to see—"

"You can see Hector tomorrow. Let's get you home and cleaned up first."

"No, I—"

"It's okay, baby." Mamá starts to soothe me while still pushing me toward our vehicle.

I try to shift out of their hold, but they guide me forward, my weak body offering zero resistance.

Jake's head pops into view briefly before he hops into the back of an SUV and disappears from view.

No! Jake!

"I—" Letting out a hopeless sigh, I deflate onto the back seat of Papá's car and stare up at the ceiling.

My eyes are burning.

Why didn't he look back and say goodbye?

We've just spent this intense time together, and yet we've been ripped apart so easily. Like a piece of bread torn down the middle, I feel soft and useless, squished between thumbs and flattened to a pulp.

"Everything will be okay." Mamá buckles up.

I shake my head. "It won't be okay."

She turns back to smile at me from the front seat. "Yes it will. Hector needs his sleep too, and you can see him tomorrow. All you need—"

"I don't want to see Hector!" I suddenly scream.

My voice is harsh and foreign, made loud by the desperation surging through me.

Mamá and Papá share a worried frown before he turns his attention to the road and drives us home. He looks into the rearview mirror and lets a few uncomfortable minutes pass before softly saying, "I know you've been through a lot, and I want to know every detail, but why don't you want to see your boyfriend?"

"I..." With a heavy sigh, I sit up, leaning forward so I can speak between the car seats. My heart is hammering so hard and fast, I'm worried I'll throw up. But I have to get through this.

"I should have told you this a long time ago, but I'm not in love with Hector."

"What?" Mamá's horrified, as I knew she would be.

My father shakes his head. "You've been through a stressful situation. Now is not the time to be making rash decisions."

"I'm not being impulsive. I—"

"You just need some sleep. That's all." Papá cuts me off, and I clench my jaw, not sure how to control the rage of emotions surging through me.

Alejandro died and he was only twenty-three. My brother was twenty-one! Life is too short, and I don't want to waste it with the wrong person. I want to be happy while I can. How can I make them understand that?

"Is it this other boy? This Jake?" Mamá asks. "Has he somehow twisted your mind? People can be drawn together in crisis, but that doesn't make it right. You can't break up with Hector. You're going to marry him!"

"I don't want to marry him!"

"*¡Estás loca!*" she snaps and then starts ranting about how crazy I am and what a good boy Hector is, how he'll make the perfect husband. I can't just break up with him out of the blue.

Her emotions grow so big and fast, it makes the car feel small. I shrink back in my seat, closing my eyes against the onslaught.

"Never make decisions when you're tired. I've told you this before," Papá clips.

When I open my eyes, he's wagging his finger in the rearview mirror, and I wish for Jake with every fiber of my being.

What would he do?

How would he handle this?

Sucking in a quick breath, I lean forward and quickly speak before I can be interrupted again. Keeping my tone sweet but firm, I gently lay out the facts. "I've been wanting to end things with him for a while now, but I didn't know how. I didn't want to let anyone down. I know how much you love him and how he filled a hole that Ademir left behind. But I can't be expected to carry that for the rest of my life. Hector is a good man, but he's just not the man for me."

"But—"

"Mamá, please, let me finish."

She presses her lips together while Papá lets out a heavy sigh.

"I know you love me and you want the best for me, and if that's true, then you can't ask me to marry someone who I don't want to spend the rest of my life with. I deserve to be happy. We all do. And Hector can't be the only source of your joy."

"You are, *mi amor*. My precious girl." Mamá starts to weep. "We don't want to lose you."

"You won't." I gently squeeze her shoulder. "Mamá, me breaking up with Hector is what's best for me."

"But he's part of our family."

"He's actually not, but I know what you're trying to say. He's become like family, and I'm not asking you to stop seeing him."

"It'll be awkward." Papá's voice is gruff with disappointment.

"I know, and I'm sorry."

Mamá pulls a tissue from her bag and starts mopping her tears. "I just don't understand. I thought you were happy."

"I thought I was too, until I met someone who…" A smile curves my lips. "Someone who made me realize that what I have with Hector is fake. He doesn't make me feel like I could fly. I can't talk to him about anything. I don't feel part of a team when I'm with him."

"Who is this boy?" Papá pulls into our driveway a little too fast, and we all lurch forward when he brakes.

I watch his fingers gripping the wheel and nearly forget it. We can talk more in the morning.

No! You've come this far. Just finish it.

"Jake," I whisper. "I've been falling for him for months. I just didn't realize. When we were together this weekend, I..."

Papá's swallow is thick while Mamá presses the tissue into her eye and starts sniffing.

"He's a good man. He's the right person for me. We've been friends for months."

"Did you cheat on Hector?" Mamá weeps.

"I kissed Jake this weekend, but I'd already told Hector I wanted to end things."

Papá huffs and shoulders open the door like he's disgusted with me.

"I'm sorry if this hurts you, but I can't carry this burden anymore. I can't be responsible for everybody's happiness. I'd be forfeiting my life for all the wrong reasons."

Papá slams the trunk closed after retrieving my pack. I wait in the car while he stomps up the steps and unlocks the door.

"Let's go, *familia!*" he barks from the porch. "Carmen, you need a shower and some rest. We can talk about this again in the morning."

Oh joy.

I slip out of the car, feeling like a balloon that's been popped and left limp on the sidewalk.

Brushing past my father, I head for the bathroom without a backward glance.

It's not until I'm under the hot spray that the tears burst out of me. They start slow, then turn into gut-wrenching sobs, eventually morphing into this weird hiccupping laughter.

I did it.

I told the truth.

And yes, it was awful, and there are plenty more horrible conversations to come.

But I made a start.

I took the first step toward getting what I really want.

As horrible as this all is, it kind of feels wonderful too.

Jake and I are going to be together, and it makes my heart flutter and sing.

37

AN INVITE HOME

Jake

MY HEAD IS POUNDING as we drive away from the airport.

Carmen was enveloped by her parents, and I didn't even get to see her before we left. She was ushered away. I tried to catch her eye, but she wouldn't look my way, so I slipped into Indigo's SUV and closed my eyes.

No one said anything on the drive back to campus.

The few times I opened my eyes, I found Brody checking on me. I'd raise my hand in a gesture of being okay, and he'd clench his jaw, then turn back to face the front. Indigo's music played softly, and I focused on the beat, trying not to think or feel.

I need a shower and my bed.

Brody and Indigo follow me into my dorm when we arrive. I let them into my room, snatch my towel, fresh clothes, and a soap bag, then walk to the showers without a word. Fifteen minutes later, I return feeling a thousand times better... on the outside.

Indigo gives me a gentle smile the second I close my door. "You want to talk about it?"

"Nope." I dump my towel in the laundry bag and avoid my brother's gaze. He's willing the words out of me, but he can take his silent stare and shove it.

I don't want to discuss anything right now.

Let me sleep.

Let me wallow.

"I'll give you a pass for now," Brody finally murmurs, "but I'm going to want a full rundown later. You scared the shit out of me, man."

His croaky voice can't hide the emotion, and I turn to face him.

What am I doing?

Shutting out the one person who's got my back?

With a tired smile, I pat him on the shoulder. "Guess that makes us even."

He grins, a surprised laugh punching out of him before he pulls me into a bone-crunching hug. I groan, and Brody lets me go as fast as he pulled me in.

"Sorry. Sorry, I wasn't thinking. I'm just so relieved you're okay." He squeezes my shoulder. "Mostly okay." He studies my face and winces.

"You should see the other guy." I try to make light of it, but he sees right through me.

His expression is pained, mottled slightly by an angry surge I know is directed at those assholes.

"They'll get what's coming to them. Justice will be served." My voice is flat, heavy with the weight of that.

Alejandro was such a good guy. I can't believe he died that way.

And poor Donita.

Carmen had a point about justice being a hollow victory. I hate to think what Donita must be going through right now. Someone has no doubt visited her home and broken her heart.

Shit. I wish I could do more.

I think about Grandpa and the only justice we managed to give him: an unmarked grave on the ridge behind the ranch. Even the thought of it makes me shudder. I've never seen it, but Brody described it in detail, needing to process the act of burying our maniac father.

Sometimes, I still can't believe he did that. He was fourteen. How is he not more broken? How did any of us survive that shit?

Indigo's staring at me with this watery smile on her face. I run a hand through my hair and blow out a breath.

"Thanks for all you did. The phone calls. The private jet."

"We would have been on it, but we wanted to leave space for you guys."

"Yeah." I nod. "Well, thanks. I mean even for coming

to the airport just now to collect me. I'm guessing you were at the ranch when I called."

Brody and Indigo share a quick look, then nod in unison.

"Everyone went out of their minds when I told them." Brody gives me a tight smile.

"Kena managed to find your location pretty fast, and we called it in as soon as we could. We managed to get through without too much trouble, and they believed us immediately because two hikers had already reported you missing. They'd been going crazy saying some guy was murdered in the woods and you were in serious trouble."

My tired brain does its best to absorb the details. "Who's Kena?"

"That would be Deeks's girlfriend." Brody grins.

"Huh." My eyebrows shoot up with surprise. "Deeks has a girlfriend?"

I don't know why I find that weird. I guess I'm just trying to compute the fact that we've all grown up and didn't see it happen to each other.

"So does Michael. They all live up at the ranch together. You really should come and meet them. It's..." He shares a look with Indy. Her brown eyes fill with warmth, and I let out a shaky sigh.

She moves toward me, gently taking my hand. "It'd be great to see all the brothers home. Even just for a visit."

"All the brothers," I whisper. That thought seems so unrealistic or surreal or something.

All the brothers home? At the ranch?

It's like a dream I can't quite make myself believe in.

"It's not the same without Grandpa." Brody shrugs, his smile kind of glum. But then he shakes his head, a light joy lifting his features. "But I gotta tell you, man… it felt like home the second I walked in that door. It was just like I remembered it, and it felt… right." He nods, obviously thinking I won't believe him. "I can't even describe it, but you should really come and see for yourself. Nell wants you back. She told me I had to tell you."

"Aunt Nell?" My voice disappears, and I'm barely able to form the question.

Nell. Sweet Nell.

She's still there?

I can't believe it. My eyes fill with tears before I can stop them.

Brody wraps his arm around my shoulders, blinking at his own tears. He opens his mouth to speak, but nothing comes out.

Indigo steps in, speaking for him. "The door is open whenever you're ready. Deeks and Michael wanted to be here too, but they respect your space. Figured the last thing you needed after this ordeal was them banging on your door. Deeks lost it when Michael suggested that, but we talked him around." She grins. "Kena's got this way of reaching him."

Brody laughs. "Yeah, she's a cool chick."

"They love you so much, Jake. They'll do anything to make things right again."

I glance at Indigo and try for a smile, but my lips are too tired to do anything but flatline. I eventually rasp a very soft "I know."

I can't say it louder than that. I don't want to promise anything, then not deliver.

But I did promise Carmen, and even if she reneges on her decision, should I go back on mine?

Nell, my brothers, the ranch. Home.

It's time for me to go back there.

As harrowing as that idea is, I'm not sure I can shake it anymore.

I hug Brody and Indigo goodbye, then crawl into bed. Flopping onto my back, I rest my arm on my forehead and stare up at the ceiling.

Grandpa's smiling face fills my mind—a crystal clear image of him making me grin.

"You know you want to." He winks at me, his deep voice piercing my soul.

"It won't be the same without you," I whisper.

"Nope. Life is designed to move forward. It doesn't matter how hard we wish for it, we cannot turn back time."

I close my eyes.

"Go home, son. Go home." Grandpa's words are the last thing I hear before exhaustion overrides all my other senses.

I wish someone was curled up against me right now. As my mind floats away, I think of Carmen and how badly I want her to come to the ranch with me.

38

THE WORST START TO A CONVERSATION

Carmen

I TOOK YESTERDAY OFF SCHOOL. I needed a day of peace where I could lie in bed and recover from my ordeal.

I checked in on Jake a couple times but didn't have the courage to call him. Our texts were friendly but not intimate. We're back to the way things were before we left. A small, disloyal part of me wondered if that was enough. If it'd just be easier to go back to what was.

My parents are still pretty cut up over my decision.

Hector came over yesterday to check on me, and everyone acted like what I said in the car was nothing, like I'd had some delusional episode. I ended up saying I felt sick and went back to bed, locking my bedroom door and hiding under the covers.

Hector stayed for another hour, chatting with my parents, before finally leaving.

I wonder if they gave him a heads-up or whether they spent the night praying I'd come to my senses.

Ugh! I have all my senses.

What is their problem?

I stop brushing my hair and gaze into the mirror, trying to put myself in their shoes. They have a daughter —their only child—who they want to love and protect. They want to support me; they're just struggling to understand. I hid my unrest for so long. I played my role so perfectly when I should have been honest from the start. It's complicated everything, and now I must face the consequences of my charade.

Finishing my hair, I touch up my mascara, then head downstairs for breakfast. It'll be weird returning to school. News of our weekend has no doubt spread among our friends. Jake attempted afternoon lectures yesterday, and his face alone would have stirred up a whole bunch of gossip. He would have handled it with a cool, calm class, the way he handles everything.

My heart flutters just thinking about him, my lips curling into a smile I can't stop.

"What's the smile for?" Mamá pulls me back to the ground.

I clear my throat and iron out my expression, taking a seat at the table as she pops a plate of freshly cooked eggs in front of me.

"Is Hector taking you to school today?" Papá sips his coffee, so obviously trying to appear casual.

"Yes." I pick up my fork and fidget with it, taking in a breath before saying, "I thought the drive down would be a good chance for me to... tell him the truth."

Utensils clatter in the sink, and I flinch, a soft gasp rushing out of me.

Papá sets his coffee down and lightly touches my elbow. "*¿Estás bien?*"

"*Sí, Papá.*" I force a smile and have to remind myself that yes, I am okay.

I can do this!

"So, you're really going to end things? Just like that?" Mamá snaps her fingers on the word *that* and takes a seat beside me, cradling her coffee mug and looking miserable.

Her eyes are puffy from too much crying, and I hate that I'm hurting her this way. It's been an emotional couple days with the tragedy, and then my heart-crushing decision to end things with a man they love.

I try to be understanding, keeping my voice gentle and soft.

"Mamá." I lay my hand on her arm. "It's been brewing for a long time. I just didn't have the courage to act. If this weekend has taught me anything, it's that life is fragile. It's vapor, so I need to make every day count. Ademir's death should have taught me that, but I was so afraid." I sniff and pull in a shaky breath. "My heart was broken. I'd lost my favorite person in the world, and I didn't think anything would ever be okay again."

Mamá's eyes well with tears and she nods, like she knows exactly what I'm talking about.

"Hector was a Band-Aid, and I used him for way too long. I wish I'd had the nerve to realize this sooner, but I didn't." My forehead bunches with apology. "I can only make from now on count, and I'm tired of being in a relationship that doesn't make me happy."

"We never knew." Mamá swipes a tear off her cheek. "Why did you not tell us?"

"I guess I was scared of hurting you or disappointing you. I know how much you love Hector."

"He's a good man," Papá murmurs.

My shoulders deflate.

"But that doesn't mean you have to marry him." He glances across the table, catching Mamá's eye before saying, "I love your mother, so very much. But it's been hard sometimes too. Marriage isn't always easy, but it would be so much worse if you weren't in it with the right person from the start. I chose that beautiful woman across the table." He points at her, his smile kind of mushy. "And I want that for my daughter, too."

"Papá." I whimper his name, lurching from my seat and wrapping my arms around his neck.

He lets out a surprised chuckle before wrapping me in his arms. Pulling me onto his lap, we hold each other tight until Mamá tuts.

"Your eggs will get cold. *Anda. Come.*"

I return to my seat, giving her a tentative smile and obeying her instructions to hurry up and eat.

Her lips are a little stiff when she returns the gesture. She's still hurting, and I need to allow that.

Scooping up my eggs, I take a small bite, not really feeling hungry, but Mamá has enough to worry about. I don't want to add anything more to the list.

After a few sips of her coffee, she places the mug down and lays her hands on the table. I glance at her face and notice she's obviously plucking up the courage to ask me something else.

My stomach pinches and doesn't release until she sniffs and taps the table with her nail. "So, tell us about this Jake."

"Jake?"

"Yes, I need to know about this man. If you're willing to let Hector go, he must be something pretty special."

A slow smile curls my lips. "He is, Mamá."

My mother's lips twitch, and I launch into as many details as I can, telling her how smart and kind he is, explaining how this wonderful person has slowly stolen my heart over time and become the man I want without me even realizing. I describe his courage in the forest and how he did everything he could to keep me alive.

Hector arrives before I'm done, and I quickly cut the conversation short.

Mamá stands, patting my hand and whispering, "You can tell me the rest later."

Papá wraps me in a hug while my mother greets Hector. He's all smiles, the poor guy oblivious to what I'm about to say.

Although, he shouldn't be. I've tried already, but this time I'll do it better.

"Good luck, *mi niña*. If you need a ride home, I'll come get you."

"Thank you."

"Hey, I'm proud of you."

I step back, emotion clogging my throat as I look at my father. He nods, his eyes glassing just a little before he pats my shoulders and sends me on my way.

As soon as Hector pulls away from my house, I get on with it. Yes, the trip will be painful, but I can't just sit here pretending for a second longer.

"Hector, we need to talk."

He grunts, gripping the wheel and shaking his head. "Worst start to a conversation ever."

"I'm sorry." I look to my hands, wringing my fingers as I get it all out. "I don't want to hurt you, but… we need to break up."

"Why?" he snaps.

I look out the window, wishing this were easier.

Just be honest.

It goes against everything inside me, but I decide to play it raw and real. "I'm not in love with you. You're a really great person, but you're not the one for me."

He scoffs, pulling onto the freeway and darting into traffic. "Bet Jake is, though, right?"

I hold my breath and count to five before calmly replying. "Yes."

"I knew you were cheating on me."

"I wasn't."

"I'm not blind! I saw the way you were together. In the forest. I'm not stupid."

"I never cheated on you. We were friends. I liked him, a lot, but I never entertained the idea that he could be more because I was with you."

"Oh, well, I'm so sorry to rain on your parade!" Each word drips with caustic sarcasm.

I look out the window, willing my courage not to fail me. If I can head-butt a full-grown man and bring him to his knees, I can do this.

Come on, Carmen!

With a heavy sigh, I shake my head. "I'm not saying you stopped me from doing anything. This is on me. I didn't have the courage to tell the truth, and I strung everybody along. I shouldn't have done that, and I'm sorry."

"Whatever," Hector mumbles.

"Please, Hector, I don't—"

"Just stop talking!" he snaps.

I do what he asks and don't say another word until we pull into campus and he parks in his usual lot near his building. It's been the worst car trip of my life, the silence icy yet suffocating.

Cutting the engine, Hector leans back with a heavy sigh. "I thought barely surviving death would wake you up, you know? You'd realize how great we are together, and all this Jake bullshit could be put to rest." He clenches his jaw. "When you told me you didn't want to be with me anymore, I couldn't face it. So I ignored you, and then I—" His jaw works to the side.

"Got kind of shitty with me," I finish for him. My insides bunch with trepidation. I'm not usually this confrontational. Worrying my lip, I hold my breath and wait for his response.

He eventually lets out a soft scoff. "Yeah, maybe I was. But I thought you were... going behind my back."

"I never cheated on you." I say it firm and slow. I couldn't be more adamant.

"Really?" He turns to me, his gaze piercing.

With a thick swallow, I softly confess, "We kissed, but not until *after* I'd told you that maybe we shouldn't be together anymore. If you'd engaged in that conversation instead of ignoring me..." I sigh and shake my head. "You know what? I don't want to play the blame game. I'm sorry if you're hurt. Truly. I never, ever wanted to hurt you, but I realized that I'd just be hurting us both by staying in this relationship when I wanted to be with somebody else." I look at him, silently imploring him to understand. "Why would I want to be with someone else if I was perfectly happy with you? Something was wrong with us, Hector. I was just too afraid to acknowledge it."

He clenches his jaw and looks away from me. His knuckles are white as he grips the wheel.

"I'm so—"

"Stop talking," he snaps, then winces. "I don't want to... hear your voice anymore. I don't want to see your face, I just... Get out of my car." His voice goes soft and wispy, his chin trembling. "Please, just... get out of my car."

I feel like someone's shoved a sword through my chest.

I want to say more, to apologize again. I've hurt him. He didn't do anything wrong, but I hurt him.

I open my mouth to speak, but he just shakes his head.

Staying feels kind of mean now, so I open the door and slip out, shutting it gently behind me.

He stays put, gripping the wheel and staring straight ahead.

Closing my eyes, I step back from his car, hyperaware that it's the last time I'll ever do that. Walking up to the college buildings, my senses are on high alert as I take in everything.

No more walking up these steps. I won't have to because my buildings are on the other side of campus. I'll never park over this way again.

My fingers shake as I grip my bag strap and picture Hector's trembling chin, his broken voice as he told me to leave him alone.

I hate so much that I've caused him pain.

My eyes burn and sting, but I don't cry. Instead I softly sniff my way across campus, not stopping my steady pace until I spot someone leaning against the wall of the building I'm supposed to be entering. His shoulder is perched against the brick, his beat-up face lifted to the sun.

The pain will be worth it.

My heart whispers those words, and I know it speaks the truth.

I'm meant to be with Jake, so I pick up my pace and close the distance between us.

39

SHE'S EVERYTHING

Jake

"JAKE!" She calls my name, and it's the sweetest sound I've ever heard, I swear.

The smile on her face melts my heart to putty. It eliminates my doubts the second it hits me, and I step away from the building, suddenly relieved that I waited for her.

Our disjointed texts yesterday left me wondering, restless, unable to sleep.

She didn't mention Hector, just said she had a challenging talk with her parents. She never elaborated, though, and I didn't have the courage to ask.

I hardly slept the night before, dreaming of Grandpa,

the ranch, Carmen, gunfire, rivers—terror and joy blended together in a heady concoction that kept jolting me awake.

I attempted classes yesterday afternoon, but I couldn't concentrate. Fielding questions about my face was a mission of its own, so I gave up and locked myself away in my room, wondering if I should even emerge this morning.

But then Carmen reaches me, wrapping her arms around my neck, and I know it's worth it.

She's worth it. Worth everything.

Her body is trembling, so I wrap my arms around her waist, wondering if she's crying or laughing or—

"Carmen." I pull away so I can get a look at her face.

She's smiling at me again, her eyes warm with... with love.

That's what it looks like.

I want to pull her in for a kiss, but...

"Hector?" I whisper.

She swallows and nods. "It's over. I told him on the way to school this morning. I told my parents, and they understand now. At least I think they do."

"You drove to school with Hector?"

"So I could break up with him."

I wince, imagining how horrible that trip must have been. "How bad was it?"

"Awful." She blinks, her voice wobbling for a moment. "But it needed to be done." She looks pale and unsure for a moment, so I touch her cheeks, gently holding her beautiful face.

"I'm sorry it was hard."

"I knew it would be."

"Are you feeling okay now?"

She nods, then lets out a little laugh. "I don't know how I'm supposed to concentrate on classes today, but..." She shrugs.

I grin, exploring her face with the tips of my fingers. "If you could be doing anything else right now, what would it be?"

Her eyebrows rise with surprise, like she didn't see that question coming. As she absorbs it, the smile on her face grows a little bigger, and then her eyes start to sparkle with a coy look that has my insides firing with desire.

"I guess I want to be finishing what we started after our plunge in the river."

My lips part, my insides turning to liquid fire.

A blush spreads across her cheeks as she lets out an awkward laugh and then asks, "If you could be doing anything else right now, what would it be?"

I gently tuck my hand behind her neck, my smile tender as I lean into her space and whisper, "This."

She meets my kiss, pressing her closed mouth against mine for a moment, before smiling and brushing her tongue across mine.

I wrap my arm around her, sealing her against me as I deepen the kiss. She lets out a sweet sound of approval, so I forget the fact that our class is starting any minute and just let myself enjoy her mouth, the feel of her body pressed against mine. Her arms wrap around me a little tighter, and she grips the back of my shirt.

"You know you guys are in public, right?" someone mutters as they walk into the building.

Carmen jerks away from me, her cheeks flaming as she looks to the ground.

I snicker and sedately peck her lips. "We can continue that later if you like."

"Yeah, I'm pretty sure we'll need to." She bites her lips together, her head bobbing like it does when she's nervous.

I love that.

I love her.

Resting my hand on her shoulder, I brush my thumb along the pulse on her neck while mine picks up a notch.

I want to tell her, but the timing doesn't feel right yet.

There's maybe something else I have to do first.

"Hey, can I ask you something?"

"Sure." She leans into my touch, her brown eyes making me feel like the most important person on the planet.

"What are you doing for Thanksgiving?"

Her forehead wrinkles with confusion and she shrugs. "It's usually a family dinner. Why?"

"Feel like taking a trip to Montana with me?"

Her lips part with a gasp. "The ranch?"

"Yeah, I was—"

"Yes! Oh my gosh, yes!" She lets out an excited laugh and barrels into me, hugging me tight and kissing my neck.

I wince at her firm hold but won't remind her of my bruised ribs in case she pulls away.

Holding her against me, I whisper in her ear, "I was so hoping you'd say that. I'm not sure I can do this without you."

"I'll be there." She squeezes me before pulling back so I can see her smile. "I'll always be there for you."

A rich emotion I can't describe whistles through me. I don't know if I want to cry, laugh, or whoop to the sky. But something inside me is humming. It's a pretty damn awesome sensation, and I want to hold on to it forever.

This girl.

She is it for me.

40

BARRETT BOYS AND BARRETT GIRLS

Carmen

IT TOOK some major convincing for my parents to agree to let me fly to Montana for Thanksgiving. Not that they really had much choice, but I wanted them to be happy about it. Thanks to a smooth visit from Jake, who calmly explained that he would look after me and bring me home safely, my parents finally relented and sent us on our way.

It helped that Castle Shaw let us use his jet again. We flew up with Brody and Indy, who had been visiting with her father for a few days. I could enjoy the private jet this second time around, and the four of us had a really great time together. Brody's got a wonderful sense of humor. He had me laughing before I could stop myself. Indy's vibrant and lovely. We talked about the fact that she's going to become a vet technician next year.

"I don't need qualifications for it in Montana. I can train on the job. I thought it'd be a good idea to try something like that for a year to see if it's what I really want to do. Then I'll look at becoming a large animal vet."

"That's cool." I smile, inspired by her motivation. Her confidence.

She looks so happy, and I get why. She's found her place, her people, and it's brought her to life. That's what she told me, anyway.

It's been good to hear, and it's helped kill the nerves of meeting this Barrett clan. I can tell Jake's nervous. His thumb rubs the back of my hand the entire flight. It's like he's afraid to let go of me or something.

As the plane lands, I catch his eye and smile. He knows I'm reassuring him, and he gives me a grateful peck on the lips. We've spent so much time together over the last month. Now that we can be together unhindered, we're using every spare minute to hang out, talk... kiss. It's wonderful. I've gotten to know him so well in this short space of time, and I feel like we've been together for years. It's such a weird sensation because I never truly felt that way with Hector.

Not every moment in the last month has been pure joy, but it's been right. It was confirmed once again when talking to Donita and describing Alejandro's final days— the way he spoke of her with such affection and love. We watched her cry on the computer screen, soaked in her smile when we told her about the trivia game and how much Alejandro loved to play

"He was smart. He knew so much." She laughed, but the sound dissolved into tears.

I blinked, my voice trembling when I told her, "He loved you more than anything."

"I know." Her watery smile reassured me yet again that I'd made the right decision in my own life. Alejandro and Donita's love was pure, strong, just like mine and Jake's. She was so grateful for our call, happy to tell us that JT and his hunting party all confessed to their crimes and were being sentenced without a trial. It's a huge relief, and even though I thought it wouldn't help, it seems to have given Donita some closure. A big piece of her heart will always belong to Alejandro, but she can hopefully move on and find love again.

Love.

I squeeze Jake's hand, grateful for every second I get to be with him. Life is too fragile to take anything for granted.

The drive to the ranch goes quickly. Brody chats away, pointing out things in the snow-covered landscape. It's kind of magical with the mountains in the distance and the sun glimmering off the white powder.

Then we drive through the small town of Harborton. It's a quaint, adorable place with a Main Street and not much else.

"This is so cute." I smile at the various storefronts, even turning to study more after we've driven past.

"That's the school Jackson goes to." Indy points to her right.

Jackson is Annie's younger brother. She's Michael's girlfriend and is a blonde firecracker, according to Brody.

"You don't mess with Annie on a rampage. Trust me. She may be little, but she's fierce."

Jake laughed when Brody said that. "Sounds like she's perfect for Michael. Is he still as mild-mannered as they come?"

"Yeah, pretty much."

Kena, Deeks... Arley?

I run through the other names, hoping I don't forget them when we arrive.

"Anything starting to look familiar?" Brody glances into the rearview mirror, trying to catch his brother's eye.

Jake nods but doesn't say anything. His cheeks have gone pale, his expression crumpled with nostalgic pain. I can tell that's what it is, because it's the same face he gets whenever he talks about his grandpa.

"It's okay." I lean over and kiss his cheek, keeping my arm around his shoulders. It's awkward with the seat belts, but I refuse to let him go until we've driven up the long, bumpy driveway and stopped outside a ranch house.

Wow. It's this amazing two-story log cabin, sitting on a rise and overlooking snow-covered fields dotted with cattle. It's a little run-down, but the words rustic and idyllic come immediately to mind. With the blue sky and sunshine, it's a glorious day, and I'm blown away by the beauty of this place.

Brody gets out of the car, and I watch Jake's hand shake as he reaches for the door handle.

"They're here!" Brody shouts, and I glance to my right, noticing two men walking side by side up from the barn.

They jolt to a stop, then both break into a run, sprinting for the car.

Jake gets out, and I slip out after him, squeezing his shoulder as he stares at his brothers. Michael and Deeks come to a panting stop beside the house, obviously waiting for Jake to close the space between them.

Making this decision was huge for him, and although he's kept in touch with Brody through texts and the odd phone call, he hasn't spoken to his other brothers yet. He wanted to do that face-to-face.

Now's his chance. It's up to him, and everybody knows it.

Running my hand down his back, I swallow and let a relieved smile cross my face when Jake walks away from me. The second he's close enough, he opens his arms wide and wraps his brothers in a tight group hug. Brody doesn't even wait a beat before bounding over and engulfing the trio with his big bear arms.

They stand in a huddle, not saying anything, just gripping each other.

Crossing my arms, I lean against the car and watch them, not even noticing the front door open until two women who look to be about my age step out of the house.

One of them's short, with wispy blonde hair, while the other is a tall Asian-looking girl. She has the cutest kid ever perched on her hip, and I smile at the toddler when they descend the stairs. That must be Arley. She's got Latino blood flowing through her veins. I can instantly tell, and it makes me feel connected before I've even spoken to her.

"Hi," Annie whispers but doesn't say more, her gaze traveling to the huddle of Barrett boys.

"How long they do that?" Arley asks.

Kena laughs. "Not sure, little one. I guess they've got some hugs to catch up on."

A boy with scruffy hair and gangly arms strolls out of the house, munching on an apple. He looks at me and smiles, but then his expression turns to a confused frown as he glances around.

"They're there." Annie points.

Jackson jumps over the railing, landing on steady feet like he's done it a hundred times before. As soon as he spots the men, he throws the apple core over his shoulder and races to join in.

His skinny arms wrap around Jake's and Michael's backs.

Annie laughs, the sound loud and merry. "Aw, he wants to be a Barrett boy so bad."

"Well, he kind of is." Indy giggles, walking around the car to stand next to me. Her eyes are misty with emotion, and she runs a finger under her lashes before crossing her arms to watch the boys. We're now in a line watching the longest hug ever known to man.

"So, what does that make us?" Annie asks. "Barrett girls?"

Kena smiles. "I don't mind the sound of that."

"Me too!" Arley lifts her arms and squeals, then glances at me, pointing her pudgy finger. "You Bawett giwl too?"

I give her a shy smile, not sure what I should be saying.

Am I in love with Jake?

Yes.

Do I want to hang out with him for the rest of my life?

Yep, pretty sure I do.

But we haven't talked about that yet.

"You Bawett giwl." Arley nods like it's definite.

"I hope so," I whisper under my breath, my eyes starting to tingle and mist over as well.

Indy hears me and wraps her arm around my waist. "If the way Jake looks at you is anything to go by, I *know* so."

Annie grins and gives me an approving nod. "Welcome to the family, new girl."

I can't help a broad smile as I dip my head and whisper, "*Gracias*."

41

HOME

Jake

THE WEEKEND HAS FLOWN BY. It's been filled with highs and lows, light laughter and heavy emotion. I know everything Deeks and Micheal went through now and was ashamed of my bitter anger toward them. But we talked that through, and they assured me I was justified. They apologized for taking off the way they did. Tears were shed, forgiveness was handed out with an ease that surprised me. I'm still kind of blown away by how peaceful it feels in this ranch house.

I'm home. It's normal, yet different... but it's home.

Michael cooked up a serious feast for Thanksgiving, and I'm so full my stomach hurts. Sitting around the table again—talking, laughing, being with my brothers—it didn't hurt as much as I thought it would. Sure, I've missed Grandpa with a physical ache, and I've avoided the fireplace like it's diseased... but this pain is eased by the noise of my family. It's kind of like old times, but it's not. We're all older, wiser. That sounds so cliché, but it's true. We've all been through some heavy shit, and it's given us depth and understanding. We all know pain and fear on this deep level, and I guess it's making us appreciate the good times. Like sitting next to my beautiful girl around a candlelit table with a fire burning in the hearth and a relaxed, chill vibe emanating throughout the room.

Arley's fallen asleep on Deeks's lap. He's brushing his fingers over her curls while he chats with Brody and Kena.

Indy's laughing with Jackson over something while Michael and Annie share a kiss.

I wish Cooper was here. It feels so wrong without him.

But he left and... who knows where he is now.

The thought sits ugly and uncomfortable in my chest, so I turn to the one thing that always makes me feel better.

Carmen's got her hand on her belly, her face scrunched in a frown of discomfort.

With a soft snicker, I lean over and whisper, "You full?"

"Oh my gosh, yes. I feel like a whale, but I couldn't stop eating. It all tasted too good."

I press my lips against her jaw. "Wanna try walking it off a little? Might make us feel better."

"Good idea." She touches my face, and we smile at each other.

"Where are you two going?" Brody asks when we start pulling on our jackets, boots, and beanies.

"We're so full we can barely move. Just going for a little walk."

"Good idea. We should—" Brody's sentence cuts off, and he leans back with a grin. "Actually, you guys just go."

Good, he picked up my *stay put* eye bulge. I love that my twin can read me so well.

Wriggling his eyebrows, he flashes me a smirk that I turn my back on, leading Carmen out the door for a little privacy.

The crisp air hits us as soon as we step out the door. Its freshness is a stark contrast to the warmth inside and I shiver, reaching for Carmen's hand as we step off the porch.

"I can't believe it's dark already."

"I know. Winters here can be a killer."

"At least we'll miss the worst of it." Carmen snuggles in next to me while we slowly walk the perimeter of the house. "I promised my parents Christmas." She worries her lip for a second, then wrinkles her nose at me. "That's still cool, right?"

"Yeah, of course. We'll catch up with my family over spring break or something."

"Maybe we could spend the summer here!" Her face lights with enthusiasm.

I pull her to a stop, taking her hands in mine. "You'd want to spend the summer here?"

"If you did." She nods. "I mean, if you still want to be with me by then."

"What?" I let out a shocked laugh, kind of appalled by the statement. "Still want to be with you? Carmen, of course I will. My God, woman, you are..." Letting her hands go, I wrap my arms around her waist and secure her against me. "You're my best friend. You're the girl of my dreams, and..." Her expression gets soft with a mushy smile. "*Te amo*."

My heart thrums wildly as I watch her face. I've been wanting to tell her I love her for weeks, but I felt like I couldn't do it until I'd settled things with my brothers.

That's done now, so I'm free.

Free to tell this amazing woman that I love her.

And I said it in Spanish too, which I can tell makes her extra happy.

She tips her head to the side, running her finger down my face and softly whispering, "That's good, because I really love you."

Our smiles press together, the warmth of our mouths countering the cold air around us. I revel in her exquisite tongue, closing my eyes and memorizing the feel of her, each little checkpoint where her body touches mine. The soft caress of her breath when she pulls back to smile at me before diving for my mouth again.

Running my hands up the back of her jacket, I'm about to deepen the kiss again when the sound of a car slowly coming up the driveway stops me.

Curious, I take Carmen's hand and lead her around to the front of the house. An SUV lurches to a stop in front of the porch steps. As my boots crunch over the dirty snow, I squint my eyes, trying to figure out who is getting out of the car.

She's tall and willowy, with a narrow face. Large loose curls cover her shoulders, tumbling over what looks like a designer winter jacket that pulls in at the waist. She looks to be in her twenties, maybe. My eyes travel down her body, taking in the expensive boots and leather gloves. I have no idea who she is until I reach her face again and something sparks as familiar.

She's smiling at me with this awed look on her face.

"Jake? Jake Barrett?"

My eyes narrow. "I feel like I know you, but—"

"Ashlyn." She touches her chest. "I'm Nell's great-niece."

No way. The chick Cooper used to make out with in the forest!

"Oh man, that's right. I remember you."

She grins, then raises her hand to wave at Carmen. "Hi."

"Oh, this is my girlfriend, Carmen."

"Nice to meet you." Ashlyn's chin has a fine point that's accentuated when she smiles. She really is beautiful. It's no surprise that Cooper liked her so much.

The light from the porch illuminates her face, and I can see the sparkle in her eyes. "I hope you don't mind me turning up like this. When Aunt Nell told me the Barrett boys were back, I had to come and see for myself." Her voice is bright and friendly.

It's hard not to warm to it, so I give her a smile and nod. "Of course. Come on in." Indicating toward the house, I head for the stairs, then turn, my smile faltering. "Not *all* the Barrett boys are back."

The light in her expression dims a little, and she softly whispers, "No Cooper."

"We don't know where he is."

She blinks and looks to the porch, licking her lips and then biting them together.

When she senses me still staring at her, she looks up and puts on a brave smile. "So how old are you guys? You must be like eighteen by now."

"Nineteen," I answer, struck by how much time has passed.

It feels so wasted, and the loss hurts.

"Time flies." Ashlyn lets out a breath, and I wonder if she's calculating how old Cooper must be. "I just turned twenty-two," she murmurs. "It's been so long since I've been back here, but Aunt Nell invited me and..." She shrugs.

I feel like there's more that she's not saying.

She's looking sad, maybe a little wistful.

"You used to come in the summer. Every year."

"Yeah." Her smile returns with the memory. "I used to love it, and... I don't know... why I stopped."

It wasn't the same without Cooper. That's why.

I can sense that's what she's thinking. Part of the reason she came was for him... and then he was just gone.

"When was the last time you were here?" Carmen asks.

"Oh, um... not for a few years. After high school, I kind

of stopped, but then I felt bad that I hadn't seen Aunt Nell in so long. I didn't have anything else to do this year, so…" She swallows, obviously not wanting to tell us the real reason. "So, I came for Thanksgiving." A smile stretches across her face, a cheerful mask. "But the cold is so not my thing." She shivers and laughs. "That's why I'm heading to a private island in the Caribbean for Christmas."

"No way."

She grins. "I know. Crazy, right? But I just need me some heat. A whole bunch of my college friends are going. Should be a blast." She shivers again, hunching her shoulders and burying her hands in her pockets. "Anyway, I better head in before my nose freezes off."

I laugh. "We'll be right behind you."

She gifts us another brilliant smile before rushing up the steps.

Carmen watches her go, and I squeeze her hand. "You okay?"

"Yeah, just wondering… was she Cooper's girlfriend or something?"

"Not sure." I shrug. "But I did catch them making out in the woods once."

Carmen's dimples appear. "I could sense that she wished he was here."

"We all do." I let out a heavy sigh.

"It's such a shame you couldn't track him down. I know Kena's been trying."

"She was lucky to find Brody. I think it'll take a freaking miracle to find Cooper."

"I believe in miracles." She lightly nudges me with her shoulder.

I glance down at her pretty smile, the surety of her gaze.

"We should have died in that wilderness, Jake. But we didn't." She wraps her arm around my waist, snuggling her head into the crook of my neck. "Cooper has unfinished business with this family. I think God wants to bring him home."

I let those words settle over me, squeezing her shoulder and kissing the side of her forehead.

I guess it is kind of amazing that the rest of us have made it back here.

Maybe Cooper can too.

Looking up to the night sky, I send up a tentative prayer of my own. I don't know who might be listening—maybe Grandpa, maybe God—but whoever's up there, I hope they can hear me.

Please, bring Cooper home.

He needs to come home.

EPILOGUE

Jake

CARMEN LEANS against me as we adjust the computer so we can both fit into the camera shot.

"Is that better?" I ask, frustrated by the internet connection.

This is the second time we've called.

"Yeah, that's looking good." Deeks gives us a thumbs-up.

I grin, happy to see his face a little more clearly. It was pretty distorted before. Hopefully this connection will work better.

"Merry Christmas!" Kena leans over Deeks's shoulder, beaming into the camera.

"Looking good, Kena."

"Thank you." She dips her hip, her Christmas bell earrings tinkling as she sways her head back and forth.

Her laughter is cute and lively. Deeks captures her chin and kisses her.

I share a look with Carmen. My brother has turned

into the biggest softy. Kena and Arley bring out his squishy side. It's... well, to be honest, it's adorable. Not that I'd say that to his face.

Carmen thinks it's the best. She was so excited about our Christmas call today. I kind of love how much she loves my family. She can't wait to get up there over the summer break, although we'll try to get there for spring break too.

Leaving the ranch and coming back to Stanford was harder than I thought it'd be. It took me a few weeks to get back into the routine of classes. But life found a way, and now I'm wishing my brothers a merry Christmas from a couch in the Díaz home. Her parents are warming to me, and I actually got a hug from her mom when I arrived yesterday. They let me spend Christmas Eve with them, and I even slept in the guest room last night. Yep, big steps.

I've been practicing my Spanish a lot, and held an entire conversation with her mother before I went to bed. She was pretty impressed. Points for me.

"So, did you get any nice presents?" Deeks asks.

"Carmen gave me a new compass and pocketknife." I hold up the goodies, stoked that she chose just the ones I would have gone for.

"And Jake bought me this necklace." She pulls her shirt collar open a little to reveal the gold cross I'd carefully picked out... with her mother's help. It looks stunning on her.

I brush my fingers down the chain and score myself a kiss.

"Kissing!" Arley's bright voice pulls us apart.

Her cute face fills the screen as she leans toward the camera. *"Fewiz Naveedah."* She practices her Spanish, making us both laugh. Carmen started teaching her a few words when we were up there and Kena was all over it, so she's kept the communication going.

"Ah. Eres una chica intelligente." Carmen tells her how clever she is. *"Feliz Navidad."*

Arley gives us a proud smile, then holds up a fluffy pink teddy bear with a white bow around its neck. "I got dis!"

"Aw, that's awesome! I love it." Carmen's voice takes on a different pitch when she's talking to kids. It's really sweet. Arley adores my girlfriend, and I can understand why. The little girl starts talking in high speed, garbling away. Something about Mr. Wabbit and how Pinky can't replace him but they can become bestest friends.

"Okay, okay." Deeks wraps up her lengthy explanation, kissing the top of her curls and passing Arley back to Kena so someone else can have a turn.

"Where's Michael?"

"He's talking to Aunt Nell. She called the same time you did. You know, stupid o'clock?" Deeks rolls his eyes.

"It's Christmas morning." Kena musses his hair with a giggle. "That's the one morning you're not supposed to sleep in."

I know exactly what she means but give my brother a sympathy wince anyway. "What time did Arley wake you guys?"

"Freaking stupid o'clock."

Carmen cracks up laughing. "Wow, that *is* early."

"Hey, guys!" Annie waves into the camera. "Michael's comin' in just a minute."

"Hi, Annie. Hey, Jackson." I wave at the screen, noticing that they're both still in their pjs. Annie is wearing a huge hoodie that must belong to my brother, but I can see her pajama bottoms as she walks away from the camera.

Jackson grins at me. "Hey, Californians. How's the sunshine?"

"Nice and warm." I tease him.

He groans, then starts complaining about how cold it's been in the mornings.

"Michael and Brody are just plain mean. It's my Christmas break and they're still making me haul my ass out of bed when it's still dark out!"

"Jackson, watch your mouth." Annie frowns at him.

"Aw, is wittle Jackson complaining about the snow again?" Brody puts on a baby voice, coming into the screen and winking at me.

We grin at each other, then start hassling our youngest "sibling." It's only fair. We got the brunt of the teasing when we were growing up. It's Jackson's turn.

He takes it like a champion and tries to dish a little back, but he's interrupted by Michael, who rushes into the room.

"I just got off the phone with Nell!" His eyes are bright, his face kind of pale.

He's agitated, but maybe in a good way?

"Baby, what's wrong?" Annie touches his cheek.

He swallows, pulls in a sharp breath then blurts, "She knows where Cooper is."

We all freeze.

What did he just say?

Carmen wraps her fingers around mine as I gape at the screen.

A muscle in Deeks's jaw twitches, his sharp features angling into a frown. "No way."

"Yes!" Michael says firmly.

"Well, where?"

"It's a private island in the Caribbean. He's working there."

"How do you know that?"

"Ashlyn called to say—"

I click my fingers. "She's there! She was going to a private island for Christmas. I remember her telling us she needed to get away from the cold."

Michael bends down to look at the screen. "Hey, Jake. Carmen. Yeah, she's there." His smile grows broad.

"With all her college buddies." Carmen nods, her smile growing too.

"That's the one."

"We gotta go get him." Brody looks to Michael, then Deeks.

My brothers have varying reactions. Michael and Brody are nodding—enthusiastic, determined.

Deeks and I remain quiet, still.

"Nell's told Ashlyn to tell him everything. See if she can persuade him to come home." Michael snickers. "If anyone can work some magic, it's her. She used to be able to persuade him to do a lot of things."

Deeks chuckles in spite of his frown.

Brody lifts his hands. "How am I the only one to not remember this girl? And why did I not know about her and Cooper?"

"Oh, come on. They used to sneak off into the forest all the time." Deeks rolls his eyes.

"I thought I was the only one who knew about that." I point to my chest. "Cooper made me promise not to tell anyone. I never did."

"I spied them once." Deeks shrugs.

Michael murmurs, "Cooper made me promise the same thing."

"Great!" Brody flings his arms up again while Indy giggles behind him. "So I was the only one who didn't know? She better get him back here so I can personally kick his butt for leaving me in the dark!" Indy's giggles get a little louder, and Brody's indignation quickly crumples. He pulls his girlfriend into a hug and kisses the top of her head. "Aw man, it'll be so good to have him home!"

"He might not agree to come." I know I'm raining on everyone's parade by saying that, but it's the truth.

He left us once. Why would he want to return?

My soft statement sobers everyone up, and I feel kind of bad about that.

Deeks rubs his mouth while Kena squeezes his shoulder.

Carmen threads her arm through mine and kisses my

cheek. "We just have to believe that she'll have the right words. You said she was persuasive."

"That's right." Annie nods. "There's no way fate can play us this hand only to slap us in the face again. We've found a link to the last Barrett boy, and he's comin' home. There ain't no two ways about it."

Michael's smile is warm with affection as he drapes his arm over Annie's shoulder and pulls her into a sideways hug.

I share a look with Deeks. I hate to be the cynical one, but I'm not alone.

I guess all we can do is hope like hell Ashlyn can get through to our older brother.

He left for a reason. Whatever that reason was has kept him away for this long.

Will it keep him away forever?

Find out if Ashlyn can convince the last Barrett Boy to come home in THE WARRIOR.

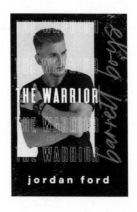

When the only woman he's ever loved drops back into his life, he comes face-to-face with a past he wants to forget. Unable to accept his shame, he's ready to walk away once more... until her life is threatened.

Cooper:
I chose one of the most remote places on Earth, an island paradise, in order to keep my past at bay. Now a piece of it has just walked through my front door. And not just any piece: an achingly beautiful, hauntingly familiar piece.

Damn, Ashlyn's sunshine smile and sparkling green eyes are going to ruin me. The connection we used to have hasn't been lost, I can sense it every time she looks at me. I so want to be the man she deserves, but it's too late for that now. There are no second chances after what I did. My only option is to walk away...until men with guns lay siege to the island.

I won't let her become another hostage.

Grandpa once said that life forced me into becoming a warrior. He told me he was proud of my unwavering fight to keep my brothers safe. But I don't think he meant for me to become a killer. Now I'm once again forced into a role I never asked for, but it's not like I have a choice.

Because if anything in this world is worth protecting... it's her.

The Warrior is the final full-length novel in a thrilling YA/NA romance series. If you like strong, complex heroes, a woman who won't give up, and a chemistry that belongs to destined lovers, then you'll devour Jordan Ford's breathtaking novel.

Buy *The Warrior* today and see how the power of love can overcome even the darkest enemy and bring a brother home.

Releasing August 2021

Sign up to receive the Forever Love Publishing emails, so you are the first to know when "The Warrior" is available.

https://www.subscribepage.com/flp_starter_library

You'll also be gifted three Forever Love Publishing books, and be eligible for exclusive teasers, sales and special giveaways.

A NOTE FROM JORDAN

Dear reader,

Writing this was so much fun. I've had this story in my head for a really long time, and I'm stoked that Carmen and Jake's were the characters I could write it with.

One thing I really wanted to do with this book is to make sure that this couple was an evenly matched team. Carmen and Jake really looked out for each other. They were both heroes throughout the story, one of them being strong when the other was weak. I adored their dynamic, and I hope you did too. They really are meant for each other and I'm so glad Carmen found the courage to do the painful thing in order to secure her future happiness.

Both Carmen and Jake had to go against their natural instinct—Carmen to stop being a total people pleaser, and

Jake to open up and forgive those who had wounded him. Those parts of this story were what gave me the big feels. I love this Barrett family and seeing them come back together as a unit. Grandpa Ray would be so proud.

Before I go, I'd like to thank my work family—Emily, Rachael, Beth, Kelé, Karen and Kristin. Seriously, what would I do without you guys?

A special mention also must go to Paz, who checked that all of my Spanish was correct. You are so lovely and sweet. Thanks for helping me out.

As always, thank you to my review team, who are still loving these Barrett boys. I can't wait to write the final book and an epilogue novella to wrap it all up.

Thank you to my amazing Forever Love Crew. I love our daily interactions. You guys make this job so fun.

Thank you to my readers and for all the love you have shown these Barrett Boys. You guys are the best!

Thank you to my family, who has walked this journey with me. We've had our own share of pain. We've had to forgive, move on, let go, but one thing that's remained constant is our unwavering, determined love for one another.

Thank you to the creator of love, the one who showed us how to do it and has been forever faithful. I love you, Lord Jesus. I wouldn't want to do life without you.

xx Jordan

LOVE146

LOVE146

END CHILD TRAFFICKING AND EXPLOITATION

A way to give back...

I am passionate about telling stories of healthy love. Unfortunately, there are some very distorted messages of what love is out in the world today, and through my books, I want to share the message of what real, good, healthy love should look like.

A way for me to show this in action is by sharing my profits with an organization that lives love on a daily basis. Their mission is to eradicate child trafficking and slavery from the world. They are truly an awesome organization, and I thank you for helping me support them.

www.love146.org

FOREVER LOVE PUBLISHING

Forever Love Publishing promotes romance fiction that is all about healthy love within families, friendships and romantic relationships. These stories will help you escape, visualize and fall in love. They appeal to both teen and adult readers who love to get caught up in a journey of self-discovery and romance.

Best-selling and award-winning author, Jordan Ford, writes high school romance with relatable characters, strong friendships, family trials and unlikely couples who discover love in the midst of tragedy and danger. If you're a fan of heartfelt romance, loyal friendships, thrilling drama and characters you can fall in love with, then check out JORDAN FORD'S WEBSITE: **www. jordanfordbooks.com**

MELISSA PEARL

the ultimate romantic adventure

Melissa Pearl is a romance author writing in a variety of genres from teen paranormal romance to small-town romantic suspense. She's passionate about telling adventure-filled love stories with relatable characters who will take you on a journey.

If you're after an escape from reality, then check out her website: **www.melissapearlauthor.com**

Lyrics of Love Novels by Melody Sweet

Melody Sweet writes coming of age romance at its best… Love is put to the ultimate test as couples at different points in their relationships are met with adversity and must find themselves in order to stay together.